Chapter 37

BY

Sidney Walker

'I waited patiently for the Lord; He inclined to me and heard my cry.

He also brought me up out of a horrible pit, out of the miry clay, and

Set my feet upon a rock and established my steps. He has put a new song in my mouth

– praise to our God; many will see it and fear and will trust in the Lord.

Blessed is that man who makes the Lord his trust, and does not respect the proud,

Nor such as turn aside to lies. Many, O Lord my God,

Are your wonderful works which you have done, and your thoughts

Toward us cannot be recounted to you in order; if I would declare and speak of them,

They are more than can be numbered.'

The Beginning

In this world where we find ourselves, we must know that despite the terrible things that we come to see and experience throughout our journey through life, there is only one King. Life gets hard, we get hit by hard blows even before we know our names, we get tossed from side to side and the course of our lives is predetermined before we even have our feet solid on the ground, but there is just one thing that is sure: The Almighty God. The effect of the hand of God when He is welcomed into a person's life makes all the difference that there is, and I have seen this for myself.

The Bible says in Jeremiah 1:5 'before I formed you in the womb I knew you, before you were born, I set you apart; I appointed you as a prophet to the nations.' What does this say to us? God has a plan for you and me! Your environment right now may limit you, make you so small and limited, and it squeezes out the life and any good you have left in you, so you say to yourself, 'there is not one good left in me' but God says no! God says, 'I know you; I know your substance, I know what you are made of, and there is so much more to you than you can see or hold on to right now.'

Now, you do not need validation from anyone around you. You do not need to be validated by your friends, your colleagues, members of your church, or even your family. The world always has so much to say; they see a man walking and wonder why he is not running, and they see a man running and say 'Hey, slow down!' This is not the type of place that you should put your worry on. The only validation that really counts for you is the one from God and He says that He knows you!

The Bible also says in Jeremiah 29:11 'For I know the plans I have for you," declares the LORD, "plans to prosper you and not to harm you, plans to give you hope and a future.' So, right now, you look at your life and you are so far from the dream you have for yourself. You have seen that where you want to get to in a few years or months, or what you aspire to be is so far off, and you are barely even halfway into the journey, so you get discouraged. I am here to tell you to get up! There is so much more ahead that you cannot see right now but it is there, and it will be yours at the right time, the God-ordained time. This is as sure as the light of day because God said it and He does not lie.

God is real, despite what the people of this world may say to tarnish His image, and He is ever-present. Life comes packed with difficulties and while this can never be completely taken out, there is one thing that the children of God will always enjoy – help from God.

God shows up for His own every single time, pulling them out of the mess they may be in, and giving them the strength to figure out their way as they go. It is a life of bliss that a majority

2

of the world is yet to plug into, and I am here to tell you about it.

Many times, in life, we find ourselves in situations that we are not sure of how to handle or what could affect others in the long run. We must never forget to think about the reactions that might come before actions take place.

For me, the color of my skin determined what my life would become. Even though I had no choice of what my skin color would be, it pre-determined where I would go, who I would live with, and who I would become. Everything was based on the brown paper bag. If you have not heard of it before, back in the 30s and 40s, the brown paper bag test determines your socioeconomic status in life. If you grab a brown paper bag and place it next to your arm, see if your skin is lighter or darker than the paper bag. If your skin is lighter, then you are more likely to be accepted into the upper echelons of society, but if your skin is darker than the bag, then you are more likely to be at the bottom of the socioeconomic order. Because my skin is darker than a paper bag, this is the way God made me. I have accepted who I am, although my pigment has been a defining factor in the lives of my mother, father, cousins, friends, and acquaintances. I am proud of who I am, and I have never let the fact that my skin is darker than a paper bag defines me. I have pushed forward.

Although, this did not happen in one day; I was beaten and pushed hard to the ground and on some days, I would wish things were different for me. But now, with the realization that everything in my life is preordained by God, the maker of

Heaven and Earth, I have learned to smile harder and bigger through it all, learning and growing into a better version of myself. Ephesians 1: 11-12 says, 'In him we were also chosen, having been predestined according to the plan of him who works out everything in conformity with the purpose of his will, in order that we, who were the first to put our hope in Christ, might be for the praise of his glory.' This gives me peace and lets me know that as long as I am in God's universe, there is a plan for me!

Back in the 1980s, a player would be a player. If he saw something he liked, his instinct would be to go for it and do whatever it took to get it, even if it was stepping outside of his marriage. If a light-skinned, red-bone sister found herself a dark chocolate man, it was a match made in heaven. Back then, it was a thing to see a light-skinned person with a dark-skinned person.

In 1984, Tyrone married a short, light-skinned, red-boned woman named Chanda. They said she was bad back in the day, but he convinced himself he had found a good one. After dating for a while, they eventually married and annulled shortly after. He could not do right by his marriage and did not want to lay his player card down.

If you were to ask Tyrone and Leyka how the child between them came along, they would give you very different stories of what took place. Tyrone's story would start off with him being with friends, enjoying his life, when suddenly the corner of his eye caught sight of a red-boned, mid-height, thick, Coca-Cola bottle-shaped 19-year-old girl.

When she was in her room, minding her own business, Tyrone took this as his opportunity to spice up the night. He sneaked, found his way into her room, and had his way with her, unaware of what would come next. Leyka's story would start with a 19-year-old girl who was minding her own business and not bothering anybody during a party her cousin hosted where she lived. When she went to her room to escape from the madness, she encountered a hungry lion who was ready to pounce on his prey. What came next was the unexpected moment of a heated one-night stand.

A little about Tyrone that you should know, he is the youngest of 6 siblings: Jim, Cathy, Janet, Matt, and Markus. Yvonne was the mother of them all, and a grandmother to me. By this time, her 6 children had blessed her with 5 granddaughters, with the 6th arriving in December of 1984. She met her first grandson in August of 1985.

Later, Tyrone found himself entangled with another light-skinned, red-bone woman from Lenoir, North Carolina; her name was Leyka. Leyka and Tyrone were solely based on a one-night fling, which resulted in my conception. During the twisted love triangle between the three, along with the marriage between Tyrone and Chanda, both of the light-skinned redbones found themselves in a war over Tyrone. Chanda was set to give birth to Tyrone's first child in December 1984, and Leyka was set to deliver his second child in August 1985. Back then, this is what a young man would call living the high life — having two different women pregnant at the same time with his child and having two different women chasing and fighting over him. This made him feel like he was living on top of the world.

Over the next several months, Leyka carried her child with grace and poise while filled with excitement. During her pregnancy, Leyka lived with different family members. While growing up and as a little child, she was born to a young mother named Robin. Robin was the oldest child in her family. Being that Robin was the eldest at 14 years old, she had to start work at a young age. She did what it took to provide for her younger siblings, which included dropping out of school and working a full-time job.

One day while walking home from work, Robin was approached by an older gentleman who offered to give her a ride home. Tired, eager, and ready to get home, she took the man up on his offer, hoping that the car ride would take her home. Unfortunately, the 43-year-old man had his way with Robin. Now, this 43-year-old man, knowing he had no business messing with a girl, even though he was already married to a wife and had children at home, chose to take advantage of the moment. Now you and I know that this man had no business messing with this child. There was a 29 or 30-year difference between the two. This dog was prying the neighborhood, sniffing out the best meal to snack on, and Robin was his target. Back in the day, during the mid-1900s, this was a common occurrence, whereas now in today's world, it is now called Statutory Rape, which is defined by statute as an act of sexual intercourse with a person under the age of consent.

Since this was not considered a crime at that time, this dog was able to get away with it, seeing that the evidence was covered up, hidden, and swept up under the table. In fact, when Robin told her mother what had happened, she was scolded and forced to keep it quiet. "You are just being fast and hot in the tail!" This encounter left a lifelong traumatic memory on Robin's mind; this is where it all started.

Nine months later, in the Detroit, Michigan area, Robin gave birth to her first-born daughter, Leyka. Like most mothers, Robin began to care for her child while working hard to take care of her siblings. Leyka became her pride and joy; nothing else in life mattered but that baby. Everywhere she went, she knew she was with the love of her life and shared precious time with friends and family.

One day, while Robin was at work, on what seemed like a perfect day, her older cousin, Shirley, who had taken a liking to Leyka, took her without Robin's permission. Erma, Robin's mother, and Shirley made an agreement that since there were a lot of kids in the home and the family was struggling already, Shirley would take Leyka and raise her in Lenoir, North Carolina. While Robin was working, Shirley grabbed Leyka along with her belongings and headed to the bus station. Since Leyka and Robin loved to take bus rides together, she assumed this was just a normal, everyday bus ride with the family, and did not see or know any difference especially because she was so young.

Some members of the community found out what was going on and wanted to let Robin know. They made a mad dash to Robin's work and warned her of what was going on. Robin immediately rushed to the bus station, knowing that she would do anything and everything in her power to get her child back — to have Leyka in her arms again. By the time Robin reached the bus station, the bus was backing out and pulling out of the parking lot, with Leyka waving through the window. Right before her eyes, her baby girl, her pride and joy, was taken away.

Robin's heart was left broken and sliced in half, knowing she would never see her child again. To make matters worse, she had no idea what her daughter would eventually think of her since Shirley made an effort to speak only of negative things about Robin to Leyka.

Living a life without her daughter changed Robin forever. She began leaning toward a lifestyle that did not benefit her health or mental state. Robin ended up meeting a married man a few years later, which resulted in her birthing her second child from him. Being that Robin was still underage and did not want to go through the same thing she went through before, the couple asked to take April, and Robin agreed to it. After this, Robin vowed to do whatever she could to not bear any future children. So, she transitioned her sexual orientation to favor only women instead of men. Because of this change, her children were not allowed to come around her or visit her. In fact, the family would send Leyka to Detroit to visit and would not tell Robin. Leyka and Tammie began to hate and have resentment toward Robin as they became adults. This was solely because of the image Shirley and Erma painted in Leyka's head of Robin, on top of the times when she was not there, and it resulted in the growing resentment.

When Leyka was nineteen, she became pregnant with her only child, a baby boy. During the pregnancy, she and Chanda continued to be at war over Tyrone. Hurt and having to deal with this pregnancy without the father of her son, Leyka built resentment towards Tyrone because he left her to go through the pregnancy alone, in addition to the image Shirley painted in Leyka's head about her mother. She always thought of the possibility of her son having the color of her skin, so she would not be reminded of her past traumas every day. Leyka constantly commented about her soon-to-be son's skin complexion, hoping he would be light skinned like her; only time would tell. Many times, friends and family would tell her if she did not want the child, they would step in and care for him because of the continued comments she made toward the unborn child.

As her due date neared, both families helped her prepare for the baby's arrival. In the hope that this pregnancy would have a positive result, meaning he would be light skinned like her, Leyka picked the name Andre for her unborn son. She held on to her son by one thin strand – the color of his skin, but God had bigger plans for him.

Chapter 0 - Birth

I was born on Tuesday, August 27, 1985, at 2:39 pm. I was a stubborn baby, to begin with, and came out feet first, so of course, my mother would give birth to a light-skinned baby boy; in fact, my skin complexion did not set in just yet. She was so excited that her bundle of joy had finally arrived. My mother named me Sidney Bernard Walker; even though she originally picked the name Andre, this is what she settled for.

Soon after, family and friends from both sides came in to see the baby without caring about Leyka's opinion. Cathy's only child, Stacey, asked the doctor to hold me by my hands and feet. Clearly, the doctor did hold me up and when he held me up in front of everyone, Stacey asked, "What is hanging down there?" This was clearly the first boy she had ever seen. Uncle Matt's comment even left the doctor, along with everyone else, leaving the room laughing. After my mother left the hospital with me in the car seat, everyone came to see me. They could not wait to hold the new baby that came into the world. They stepped in where they could help Leyka out, knowing that she was a new mother. She eventually found a small but quaint place off a quiet country road in Lenoir.

Thankfully, a lot of family members lived close by, so if she ever needed anything, someone would be there to help.

Toward the end of the first year of my life, my mother noticed that my skin color began to change and transition from lighter to darker. This was not what Leyka wanted. Rather than choosing to love me regardless, no matter what I looked like, she resented me for the dark color of my skin. Even though her mother and my father were dark-skinned, she wished that her son would share the same skin color as her. Because of the struggling relationship, she endured with her mother, as well as the painful pregnancy and neglect she received from Tyrone, the emotional turmoil she felt was bestowed onto me.

Chapter 1 – First Birthday

My first birthday was on Wednesday, August 27, 1986. I was an ambitious baby, especially since I began to crawl and walk before I turned a year old. My mom would find things for me to do so I could keep busy. Want to know the best part? A cousin in the family gifted me with a German Shepard puppy! We named him Cocaine, mostly due to his energetic personality. Cocaine and I became the best of friends, constantly entertaining each other while Leyka and her friends hung out and had a great time. Now let's be real; who in their right mind would ever name a dog Cocaine? Looking back, I am not sure what I would have named the puppy, but certainly not Cocaine.

On any normal day, you never know what could happen. For me, Cocaine went missing. I was crying hysterically, and my mom was unsure of what had happened. She got the picture when she noticed Cocaine was not around and began searching around the area to try and find him. Cocaine was nowhere to be found. When you lose a man's best friend, it can be incredibly hard on the child. But as time passed, I stayed with family more often, which helped me let go of Cocaine. Although I will always remember him, the pain got easier each passing day.

Mom and I continued to live life with all its ups and downs. She was still upset that she was left to raise me on her own. To help alleviate some of the stress and anxiety she was experiencing, I would stay with her family and friends from time to time. We had to do what needed to be done to help our family survive. But over time, Leyka's uncle, Craig Shell, and his wife, Sherrel Lee, and Leyka's cousin Shelly, were willing to help, take me in, and help raise me because they shared a common love for me. As a part of their family, they wanted to make sure I knew I was loved by them.

In the meantime, Tyrone and Chanda continued to battle through their ups and down. It even came to the point where Tyrone and Chanda separated, leaving Chanda pregnant with her third child. After finding out the news, they both did whatever they could to reconcile their differences. But in the end, it did not turn out for the best. While they were trying to work things out, Leyka thought that this would be the time for her and Tyrone to reconnect and work things out. But when she saw Tyrone was doing everything, he could make it work with Chanda, Leyka's frustration and resentment toward me grew to a new level.

Tyrone worked at a vinyl warehouse in Hickory. One night before his shift, Leyka and Tyrone got into a massive argument, leaving her pissed off at him. The next morning, "sleep it off" did not occur to her, and still pissed after the argument last night, she took me to where he works at, sat me in his car, and left me in the mid-summer heat. She knew she had no business leaving me in the car when during this time, temperatures peaked in the low 100s. Not even up to two years old at the time, I was left alone to fend for myself, even though we all know a 1-year-old could not do anything to protect itself, for several hours before anyone noticed I was there.

Eventually, one of Tyrone's coworkers saw me sitting in the car and threatened to call social services. Pissed and unaware that I was even there, he begged his coworker not to call social services and instead let him take me to his mother, Yvonne's house. When we got there, she welcomed me with open arms, relieved to know I was okay. Not willing to see her first grandson go without her, she did what she would to show me love unconditionally. Already living with Yvonne was her oldest daughter, Cathy, Cathy's husband, and Cathy's only child Stacey, in a two-bedroom apartment in East Hickory.

Once Tyrone got off work, he picked me up from grandma's house and went to my moms with the hope that she would take me back with her, but she was not having it. She wanted nothing to do with him or me. Unfortunately, she was not having it and wanted nothing to do with either of us anymore.

This was the start of what I could sense as rejection in my life. The Bible says in Psalm 27:10 *'When my father and my mother forsake me, then the LORD will take care of me.'* So little did I know that this was going to be my own reality. At such a young age, my mother decided that she did not want a dark-skinned baby, and with this unfair prejudice, she held grudges against my father and made sure that I paid for it, not minding how young and innocent I was. I was feeble and weak, having no one to hold on to and no one to defend me when I cried for help, but God showed up for me and changed the narrative of my story.

Chapter 2

It is Thursday, August 27, 1987. Another year had passed, and Leyka and Tyrone never reached a solution. I am two years old now, and Yvonne began to ask more frequently about taking me in under her wing because of what was going on. She wanted me to be able to stay with her so I could have a consistent place to call my home instead of flipping back and forth between different people. But due to the number of people living in the apartment already, there was really no room for me to live there.

By this point, Tyrone had had it with Leyka; he was done with the Back and forth. Thankfully, they finally reached some sort of agreement, and Tyrone finally convinced Leyka to keep her son. Leyka kept me for a couple of weeks before she and her lover at the time dropped me off on grandma's back porch. Without any warning, Yvonne had no idea her grandson was sitting on the back porch. Her next-door neighbor ran out of their house and yelled, "That girl left that baby sitting on your back porch!" She rushed to the back porch, knowing that Leyka had left the baby sitting in the heat once again.

As they gathered my things, Yvonne called Tyrone and begged him to let her keep me. I was her first grandson, and she could not stand to watch me go through all the pain and confusion at my little age. She became overprotective of me and did whatever it took to make sure I had what I needed, but Tyrone saw me as a burden to his mother and would not let me stay with her.

By this time, Tyrone and Chanda had separated, and he had his own place. To make matters easier, Tyrone told Yvonne that he would drop me off at her house while at work during the day and pick me up on the way home.

After doing this back and forth for a while, Tyrone struggled with balancing working and being a single parent. One day, Yvonne told Tyrone that a bad storm was coming; he went to the store to stock up on some beer. When the storm came, it was a rough night. Because I would not stop crying, he tried to put me to bed, but nothing worked. Rather than being patient and trying to find a way to get me to stop crying, he instead beat me and left me alone in a room. Eventually, he came to get me and put me in bed with him, and the storm was gone when I woke up.

When we woke up the following day, there was a very large tree on top of the apartment building, along with several cars in the parking lot. Because of the tree, we had no power. Tyrone found out that Yvonne still had power, so he dropped me off there. At this time, Tyrone realized how difficult it was going to be to raise a child on his own. Trying to work and be a parent became overwhelming for him. He realized that his party life, working full-time, and raising a child would just not mix. By this time, he decided to let me live with Yvonne because he knew she would do all she could to raise me right despite what I had already been through. Yvonne did what she could for the rest of her life to raise her grandson to the best of her ability, fighting tooth and nail every step of the way.

On the other hand, not everyone was welcoming of this decision. Cathy and her husband, Kevin, felt that the apartment was already overflowing and that adding a two-year-old would bring more stress to everyone living there. This would just add more fuel to the fire. But that was not going to stop her from doing what she needed to raise me. She was determined she would not see me go without the help I needed.

Chapter 3

Another year, another unexpected adventure. I am three years old and still living with my dad's mother and family; everyone had to adjust to me living in the apartment with them. Leyka had fully removed herself from my life, and Yvonne, already raising two grandchildren, became protective. One day, Kevin wanted him and Stacey to hang out. When hearing this, Yvonne felt that something was not right but could not put her finger on it. This had been occurring more often than it should. Kevin always wanted to be alone with Stacey. Yvonne tried to warn Cathy, but she refused to believe that her husband, the man that she loved, would do something like that. She was not having it and told Yvonne that what she said was ridiculous and ignored her. This added more fuel to the fire. Yvonne believed something was happening that shouldn't be, and Cathy continued to live in disbelief.

If nothing could add more stress, bills for the apartment began to rack up. On top of that, the added expense of another child added more undue stress. This led to everyone trying to find ways to cut back and save money; for example, we cut back on the water bill.

When I turned three, the family asked Kevin, the only male there, to show me how to take a bath. At that time, I did not know what was going on. Once in the bathroom, Kevin would lock the door because I would always keep trying to get out. I cried, not understanding what was happening. Eventually, I calmed down and began to play with my toys in the water with Kevin. After a few months of having bath time with Kevin, things changed. During a bath, Kevin was washing my back and took this as his moment of opportunity by placing himself in between my bottom and my legs. I had no idea what was happening, and I froze.

At 3 years old, I did not know if this was something I should be okay with or something that I should be afraid of. He told me to squeeze my two legs together as he slid himself in-between my legs, getting himself off to the stimulation.

I had no idea what was happening. This was just the start of what happened behind closed doors. Things advanced when Kevin persuaded me to slide himself into my mouth. As things continued, no one knew what was happening. And as a naïve child, Kevin told me not to say anything to anyone; we were just 'playing.' He took advantage of me, but I did not know this at the time. In addition to me, Kevin had also been taking advantage of Stacey. Kevin was straight, so who would ever think or believe that he would dare do anything like this to me? Yvonne had her suspicions that something was happening between him and Stacey but could never prove anything.

This continued until Kevin got tired of Yvonne blaming him for something she could not prove. She never actually saw it happen. This brought fuel and separation between Cathy and Yvonne. Cathy was tired of being pulled between her mother and husband. It was time for the family to get a place of their own that offered more privacy. This was something Yvonne saw that she knew was not going to be beneficial for Stacey. This also allowed him to have his way with her where no one could stop or intervene. Both Kevin and Cathy found a 3-bedroom house about 15 minutes from Yvonne. Being that Yvonne did not drive, this would prevent her from just popping up at their home without letting them know. She also did not agree with the couple's religious beliefs. They chose to become Jehovah's Witnesses, which caused a huge divide between the families.

Yvonne was someone who loved cooking large family meals for Sunday dinner. There was nothing like everyone gathering at grandma's house for Sunday dinner. One thing's for sure, Yvonne was the queen of soul food cooking: fried chicken, mac and cheese, green beans, corn, rice, beans, ham, pig feet, pork chops, roast, lemon pound cake, anything you would imagine would be in a southern meal. Sundays brought all of her children and grandchildren together. Other friends and family came and joined in for Sunday meals. She never turned anyone away. If you were hungry, she would make sure she had food for you to eat if there was nothing else. She never liked people to go hungry.

Chapter 4

When a person finds a path in life, it will always pay that they identify if this path is right or wrong for them, or if it aligns with the future they desire. If you find yourself on a path and see that all this way does is steal from you; steal your peace of mind, steal your comfort and happiness, or steal your sanity, then that is the wrong one for you. But if the path you are on keeps you on a constant slope of growth, challenges you to be better, to do things the way that God intends for you to do them, and makes you happy, then, you should be rest assured that you are on a safe track.

This was the case for me while I was growing up. The life I had with Yvonne was a very important path in my life, and it was ordained by God. Yes, it did not give me the best kind of feeling to see my parents juggle me between one another and have constant fights and bickering on who would keep me, but each time I think back, I say to myself 'God allowed.' Only God knows the future from the beginning, and He alone knows what would have become of me if I lived full time with my mom or dad, or worse, both together. He knew all that could come of it, so he made my path led to a life with Yvonne. I did not know it back then, but everything about my life with Yvonne was planned by God to give my life great meaning. Yvonne was placed so strategically in my life to give it the meaning that I never would have found in the environment of Leyka and Tyrone. Many practices that have kept me afloat in the storms of life, Yvonne taught all of it to me. She was a woman who feared the Lord and she ensured that everything she believed in, she trained me in that same way.

The Bible says in Proverbs 22:6 *'Train up a child in the way he should go, and when he is old, he will not depart from it.'* Yvonne knew this, and not once did she let me just live as I wished to. She brought me up in the right way and enforced it too until my little mind began to grasp the need for it all. She knew that she was an instrument in the hand of God to mold me into a great man and she did not take this important assignment for granted.

Going to church with the neighbors, Sadie and Brook, was something I enjoyed. Sadie lived at the end of the apartment complex. She was raising a young girl named Brook. In my case, the saying "It takes a village to raise a child" would really be set into place. Several people in the neighborhood attended Bright Star Church. Again, the scripture in the Bible, Proverbs 22: 6 that says, 'Train up a child in the way he should go, and when he is old, he will not depart from it' begins to come into play. At 4 years old, I loved going to church and singing in the choir. It became one of my favorite pass times.

Often, you would see the children play in the front yard in the apartment complex as well as at church. They would take turns acting like the different people in the church, like the pastor, the ushers, and the choir members. It was something the children often did. To me, it showed that what we saw was being ingrained in our hearts and forming the foundation of our personalities. It was showing us how to live, and how to act, and I am beyond glad that the 'view' that God placed in front of me to emulate was one worth having. It made me the great man I am today, showed me how to tackle problems in a way that glorifies and acknowledges God, and surely, this is the best way to live.

The next-door neighbor, Rita, became very close with Yvonne—basically almost like sisters. The two of them would sit on the back porch and sometimes talk from sunup to sundown about anything and everything. Rita had 6 children who would also come and visit from time to time with her grandchildren. They also attended Bright Star Church for many years.

Both families would often end up at either mom's house at the same time. This allowed for all the kids to play together. There was nothing better than seeing a large group of children playing in the front yard. Sometimes, the children would get together with the other kids in the neighborhood and play kickball, and it was nothing like a good old game of kickball. Kids would come from everywhere to come and have some fun.

Across the field lived Yvonne's sister, Harriet, her husband Bill, their son Kurt, and Rickman, Harriet's oldest son. Harriet worked in the local hospital, and Bill worked at the local mill around the corner. They also had a black dog named Lady. She was the neighborhood dog and was loved by everyone. Bill was also known as having that good old back-in-the-day white liquor that came in the milk jug moon shine known as Bulk. You knew it was a good day when they had to help Bill get into the house. Many came from far and near just to get a drink from Bill.

Yvonne's boys stayed at Harriet's to drink and carry on. Sometimes it was never a dull moment across the field. The young guys in the family often tried to outdrink the old heads. This carried on for many years.

After a few months, I started school at Blue Bird Elementary School. I loved my kindergarten teacher, Mrs. O'Neal. She became a mother figure to many of the children in her class by doing what she could to help train them up and get them what they needed. One day in school, there was a pretty girl in the class, and I was given a chance to sit beside her. I was going to make her my girlfriend. She was really skinny, had long, pretty hair, and had a dress on that day. It was movie time, and the lights went out. Being as young and eager as I was, I was excited about this pretty girl in class. When the lights were out, I snuck my hand under her dress while everyone was looking at the movie. I did it slowly but surely, and I worked my way up her dress. *"Wow, this is what it's like,"* I thought to myself; then, like a hawk, this angry black lady shot across the room and grabbed me up.

By this time, I am confused about what's going on since we were just trying to have a little fun. She took me to the back room, pulled out her paddle, and went to work on my bottom. She was not playing around, and she wanted me to know that I was wrong. Let me say I learned my lesson that day: Never stick your hand up a girl's dress. Mrs. O'Neal also put me in time out to let me think about what I had done. She explained to me what was wrong and that I had no business with my hand under her dress.

Now, you may be wondering or thinking what a young boy not up to five years of age was doing under a girl's skirt. You may be wondering what was going on in my mind, and what kind of thoughts I was processing in my head when I was still so young. The Bible says in 1 Corinthians 15:33 *'Do not be deceived: "Evil company corrupts good habits.'* No matter how much cleansing a person's mind undergoes, as long as they keep returning to the mud, it will get dirty again. Yvonne did a great job pulling me out of the mess that was my father's house and my mother's house too, but she had no idea what Kevin did to me. The few days I often spent away from her at my dad's place was the 'mud' that stained the work Yvonne was doing, and my mind was a sponge, soaking it all in. We have been told as Christians that if we spare the rod, we spoil the child, and God allowed for my teacher at the time, Mrs. O'Neal, to be strong in her disciplinary moves. If she did not care about whatever we did or she said 'oh, he is just a kid, he will come around eventually', nobody knows what would have become of me. This was yet another plan of God that was working for me even when it looked like everything was against me. She disciplined me and made me know that I was wrong. That was the last of such a chapter in my life.

A few days passed, and I was with my best friend, Adam C. We played and always hung out together. He was the first person that I called a best friend; realistically, he was more like a brother to me. We often hung out on the playground. We never got to hang out outside of school since Yvonne was quite overprotective and would never let me go to anyone's house.

It was the fall, and I became very ill. Not knowing what was going on, Yvonne took me to the doctor, only to find out that I had double walking pneumonia, which was very serious for a kid my age. I was very weak, and my doctors did everything they could to help me get well. It took several weeks to get me back to where I needed to be. Due to my sickness, I missed several weeks of school. Yvonne allowed Adam C. and my cousin, Traci, Janet's only child, to come over and play with me. This helped me heal and get strong again. After a few weeks of being home, the doctor released me to go back to school.

A few weeks after being back in school, there was a kid in the class named Kyran. During class, we got into a fight, and Mrs. O'Neal took us to the back room, paddled us, and forced us to apologize to each other. She let us know that we shouldn't be doing things like that and that we needed to make up and be friends. Yet, another training for Mrs. O'Neal. You see, like I said, God will always take care of his own. God was intentional about the plan he had for me; He had set me aside for greatness and starting off at my very young age, he put experiences that may have seemed like obstacles in my way, all to train me and prepare me for the life ahead. The sickness could have taken my life, but it did not. It was bilateral, and so, both of my lungs were infected. This did not stop God from taking charge of it all and curing me completely.

As time passed, the winter season came to an end. The flowers bloomed, and the kids were outside on the playground playing again. It was a nice, sunny day, and the children were outside playing. It was almost the end of the day, and it was time for the kids to line up. As the teacher blew her horn, everyone raced to see who could get into line first. Children jumped off of slides and out of swings; it was a mad dash to see who would get there first without knocking down the teacher.

As I ran to get in line, I was struck in the head by a swing, which knocked out cold for a few minutes. Mrs. O'Neal raced over to aid me and checked out where the swing hit my head. There was a very large knot coming up on the back of my head. "This doesn't look good." Mrs. O'Neal said. They took me back up to the classroom, placed an ice pack on it, and laid me in the back room until it was time to get on the bus. Still not feeling well the next day, Yvonne decided to keep me home from school. The knot still was not going down. Yvonne's hopes were that after a few days, it would go away.

A whole week passed, and things were still not looking good. Yvonne sent me back to school, but I continued to complain about head pain. By this time, Yvonne called the doctor, and they ordered to have x-rays done. After several tests and x-rays, the doctor recommended that surgery would need to be done. The results showed that there was pressure on my head with fluid as well as a skull fracture. Their hopes were that once they released the fluid, the fracture would heal itself.

Struck by the information, Yvonne instantly began to prepare for the surgery. She reached out to Tyrone and Leyka and asked them both to be there for me. She planned the surgery a week out so they could have time to prepare. This was going to take me out of school for at least 6 to 10 weeks. She realized this was going to be a long journey for me, but she wanted to make sure this was something that I would not have to worry about.

It was surgery day, and Yvonne depended on my dad to show up to take me to the hospital, but he was missing in action. Leyka's uncle, Craig, and his wife agreed to meet everyone at the hospital. Once Yvonne did not hear from Tyrone, she called Craig and his wife, and they agreed to take us both to the hospital. Craig stated that he would not miss this for the world. "That's our boy, and we love him," Craig said. We arrived at the hospital and checked in. I began to ask where my mom and dad were, and Yvonne comforted me and told me not to worry. She helped me get ready for surgery and continued to let me know everything was going to be alright.

While in the prep room, Tyrone showed up, and Yvonne gave him the eye to let him know that he should have been here way before the time he arrived. Now you know when your child is in the hospital, the assumption would be that either parent would rush there to make sure they were okay. Apparently, this did not occur to Tyrone or Leyka. Even after Leyka promised she would be there, she was nowhere to be found.

Rejection was the norm for me as a child, I could not get over it and my parents did not care much about the effect their lifestyles had on me. I felt a void in me, a deep void of having no father or mother to care about the matters concerning me.

They did not care much about my feeding, my schooling, the clothes I wore, or even my growth. I was a growing child, and you would think that my parents would be excited to see what was becoming of me, but this was not the case. The Bible teaches in Psalm 68: 5 that God, in His holy habitation, is a father of the fatherless, a defender of widows, and if my mother or father knew this, they would have had a different outlook on life. Luckily for me, Yvonne knew this, and she instilled this wisdom in me, so that each time I felt incomplete, I would recall that I had a father and mother in God, through her.

By not wanting to make a big deal about my father's lateness and my mother's absence, she did not say anything to him about me. Although she was pissed, she was happy that he showed up. As the doctor showed up to prepare the family, it was time for them to wheel me back. This was heartbreaking. I began to scream and cry because I had never been taken away from my grandmother before, and this was just as hard for me as it was for her. Not understanding what was going on made matters worse. She walked as far as they would allow her to go, but I began to scream and fight, wanting to be with my grandmother. This was hard and very overwhelming for us. Not having it, the doctor was not able to help me calm down. They would have to let my grandmother come back with me until I was asleep. Eventually, they started the surgery and finished with no complications. By that time, you would think that Leyka would have shown up, but she was a no-show once again. Sadly, but true, this was an ongoing process and happened more often than it should. But it was to be expected.

Everything went well a few weeks after the surgery. Unfortunately, the surgery left a scar on the back of my head that would be there for the rest of my life.

During the next several weeks, I was not able to play outside. Yvonne kept a close eye on me, making sure I would not hit my head up against anything. Often, I would ask if I could go out and play, but it was, more often than not, a no. Sometimes when there weren't a lot of kids outside, she would let me play or sit on the front porch, but because of the injury, she had to keep a close eye on me. This carried into summer.

Chapter 5

I could not believe it – it was time for me to officially start first grade. This was also the first time I've been around a lot of kids since the surgery. Yvonne asked my new teachers to keep an eye on me to make sure I was well taken care of. She was like my guardian angel, my gift from God. The last thing that needed to happen was for me to be bullied and hit in the head.

Most of the kids in my class noticed the line on the back of my head. Someone in the class stood up and yelled, "Who don' mess your head up!" The children around began to crack jokes. This was an ongoing thing over the course of a few months. I did not understand why kids would call me names. It got so bad sometimes that I begged my grandmother to let me stay home. Yvonne had to force me out the door to get me to school. She did not and could not understand what was going on. The kids in my class would call me anything from skid marks to gappy because of the scar on my head, which then led to comments revolving around my skin complexion. I never really understood why the bullying became something about my skin complexion, but it led me to want to avoid school altogether.

When Christmas vacation arrived, I finally got a break from all the bullying at school. Yvonne did all she could to provide for her grandson. She depended on her children to take care of me. I was like the younger brother of all the children. On the Sunday before Christmas, I saw Matt come across the field from Harriet's.

Since I was Matt's go-to target to harass, I immediately took off running. Unfortunately, I was no match for Matt because he found me within minutes. Knowing I could not beat him, he grabbed me by the feet and turned me upside down. I fought with all my might as tears flowed down my face. Yvonne yelled, "I told you to sit down somewhere! You always want to start playing around." It was never a dull moment between us; we would go at it for hours.

The next time Matt came over, Yvonne told me to sit down and stay still. Matt, being his normal self, started picking on me as usual. She grabbed the switch and hit Matt with it. However, that did not stop him. He grabbed me by the foot and turned me upside down with my hands almost touching the floor. I swung my arms to try and hoist myself up and over Matt to get away from his grasp.

"Put him down!" Yvonne yelled at Matt, but this only egged him on. He continued to tell everyone I was going to be gay, so he picked on me harder without hesitating even once. Everyone in the house cried and laughed as they witnessed what was happening. To top it off, Matt made fun of my Ninja Turtle underwear, which brought me over the edge. This was an ongoing thing between us.

It was not a reason for me to be constantly sad, and now that I think of it, it was just fun and games.

Chapter 6

Another year came, but the bullies in school remained the same. The only thing that changed was they became more creative with their tactics. Often, the children in school smacked me in the back of my head for no good reason. Yvonne tried to keep my hair low cut, but it seemed to have made things worse. Markus R., our family friend and barber, cut my hair for years. But at one point, Markus R. had my cousin Clifton and me fighting one another for no good reason. Eventually, I no longer wanted Markus R. to cut my hair, but I had no other choice. This would go on for several years.

Matt's child's mother, Shay, decided to hold back her daughter, MaShay, in the first grade. Not only did they decide to hold MaShay back, but Chanda chose to hold Danielle back in the first grade. So, Traci, Janet's only child, was only a year behind us, but when we were all held back, this put us all in the same grade.

So now, the bullies at school had another reason to pick on me more because I was forced to be held back for a year. No matter where I went, they were there. I could not even go to the bathroom without hearing them call me names. I hated going to school. Because not only did I have this issue to deal with, but

I also struggled with a speech impediment—a bad slur. No one was sure where it came from, but they assumed it originated from me sucking my thumb. I went to speech therapy to try and fix it, and over time it helped me articulate what I was saying more clearly to people.

To add to the list of problems, I also struggled with a writing problem. Originally, I was left-handed and wrote backward instead of forward, which was strange since it was something I had worked on for a while. My school's guidance counselor, Ms. Lopez, was a wonderful resource for Yvonne and me. She found and placed me into a Big Brother Program that made a huge impact on my life. Since Yvonne was getting up there in age and was not able to do as much to help me, in addition to her health issue, the Big Brother Program was a great next step for me. As a part of the program, I was assigned a Big Brother who served as a mentor and tutor for me. We did different outdoor activities, and he helped me with getting supplies for school as well as paying for field trips.

Now, this program may have just been a regular initiative to every other person, but to me, it was a very important highlight and my growth and development. My writing and speaking problems would have been big enough to dim every light that God placed in my life. I was already dealing with bullying and rejection, which are quite heavy; heavy enough to kill and destroy every ounce of confidence, self-esteem, and value for the person I was. A problem with speaking and writing made me feel like I was an unlucky person. The bullying increased, and a few times, I would wish that I could close my eyes and wish it all away. The Bible says in Proverbs 13:20, *'He who walks with wise men will be wise, but the companion of fools will be destroyed.'* The Big Brother program gave me direct access to a table filled with wise people. I was in constant contact with people who wanted me to be better, people who loved me genuinely as God loves me, and people who wanted only the best for me at all times. If you can't see it yet, I will remind you – my life was preordained by God, and so is yours. God sits in the heavens, yet the earth is his footstool, and he sees all that happens day in and day out. He will go any length necessary to see that his will in your life and mine is done, so when the devil throws things at you, rather than cry and worry, smile and be hopeful! Remember the story of Jesus? 1 Corinthians 2:6-8 says *'However, we speak wisdom among those who are mature, yet not the wisdom of this age, nor of the rulers of this age, who are coming to nothing. But we speak the wisdom of God in a mystery, the hidden wisdom which God ordained before the ages for our glory, which none of the rulers of this age knew; for had they known, they would not have crucified the Lord of glory.'* The devil tried and tried hard to cause the downfall of man by pushing for the persecution of Jesus Christ. When he finally turned the hearts of many against Jesus and caused them to crucify Him, he thought he had Jesus under his control forever, but the wisdom of God is far ahead. It is far ahead of what any man may think is the best or highest level of wisdom. God turned everything around and made the death of Jesus purposeful, even the best thing that has ever happened in the history of Christianity.

I saw these signs in my life too, so the things that the devil thought that he was using to pull me back and pull me down,

God would use that same thing, in the same breath, to pull me up. That was the hand of God in my life, and still is to this day. The big brother program was so significant that it turned my zero to one hundred in no time, even Yvonne saw this.

I had not seen my mother, Leyka, for several years now. I even asked for her to speak with me over the phone a few times, as she made big promises that she would see me and bring me things. This was an ongoing occurrence, but nothing ever came of it. Even Yvonne was tired of the lies and continued to be there as a support system for me. Not only was she dealing with my mother not stepping up to the plate, but Tyrone also found himself a new girlfriend named Reba.

As a result of this new relationship, his attention for her went from 0 to 100, and his attention for me was nonexistent. He fell short of me and decided to put all of his attention on his expectant third child with Reba. But like every other relationship he had, they both went through their rollercoaster of ups and downs. A few weeks passed, and Tyrone was jumped by a group of young boys. Now some say that one of the boys had beef with him and others believed that Reba set it up. Tyrone's siblings weren't having it and demanded that he leave Reba alone. His being jumped could have taken his life.

When I needed to get away from stress at home or school, I went to church for comfort. At church, one of the mothers, Mrs. Monday, asked to be my Godmother. She took a liking to me since I started showing up at church, and she was always there to make sure I had what I needed. Not only had Mrs. Monday stepped in, but Mrs. Essie also stepped in to make sure I had everything I needed. Many other church members stepped up to help as well by sponsoring Christmas and other things I needed or wanted. The church was my home, my true home. It was even better that Yvonne introduced me to Christianity and also approved of it. The love that I never experienced from my parents, I was given in multiple folds by various members of the church. For me, it was the family of God, and they were also so intentional in extending the love of God to me. So, I really did not miss out on the feeling of true and undying love.

A few weeks passed, and the family was visiting Yvonne's for dinner. It was late in the evening, and all her children were present, having a good time. But as they say, every good thing must come to an end. Reba showed up to talk to Tyrone, but the family did not have it. One thing you do not do is mess with any of Yvonne's children. Yvonne did her best to refrain and stay in the apartment, but she was so pissed that this girl had the audacity to show her face. Yvonne's children, one by one, went after her, but that did not stop her from standing her ground for the baby she was carrying. It got so bad that the police pulled up and right back out, choosing not to care. The only thing that was stopping the family from putting their hands on Reba was Tyrone. After a while, the tension calmed down, and everyone went their separate ways.

Chapter 7

This was the year for change. The church really stepped up and into place, helping Yvonne wherever they could. I was now in the second grade and had improved a lot. Yvonne continued to strive to teach me the ways of life, opening my eyes to what the future lay ahead. Job 12:12 says, *'Wisdom is with aged men, and with length of days, understanding.'* Yvonne was wise and she had understanding too. If anyone spends some time with her, they could tell that she had hacked the God's way to live life. More than anything, I am glad I had her showing me the way to go from a very young age. She allowed God to lead her, and with the wisdom she acquired, she lived well and led me too. She did not lean on her own wisdom, rather, she looked up to God in everything that she did and taught me to do the same. These are valuable lessons that will never leave my heart because they were used in my foundational years. I do not know how she did it, but she made me see the use and importance of inviting God into all I did – from my feeding to my games, my educational endeavors, my personal needs, and even as little as starting my day.

The next day was Sunday, and Yvonne and I enjoyed our normal morning routine, Johnny Jones Gospel. When the show came on, Yvonne played the role of the choir, and I played the role of Choir Director. This was one of our favorite shows to watch every Sunday at 9:00 am and 9:00 pm. Going to Bright Star Church was nothing like going to normal, everyday church. Singing in the choir or even on the usher board was something that made a positive impact on my life. Most of the people in my family did not attend church. Yvonne sometimes attended church with me on special holidays like Easter; we had a wonderful time.

The choir I sang in for the past few years was celebrating an anniversary, which they had been preparing for a few months. This was an exciting event like Johnny Jones Gospel Live and in-person. People came from near and far for the celebration. The choir practiced their step down to march in the church, which was a fan favorite for whoever attended.

It was a few days before service, and Yvonne went out to make sure I had my attire for the concert. The choir was wearing its traditional blue and white color combination. The music that the children's choir prepared was similar to that of the adult choir.

The choir has been together for many years and always packed each church they performed in. They were very well known for their singing, and they did not mind praising God and His word. I always thought this was one of the choirs off of Johnny Jones Gospel. This was happening a lot in the area, and Bright Star was known for its choir's anniversary. It was a major impact on the community. Many souls were saved by their beautiful music.

Yvonne was a role model to me, especially when it came to helping me to learn how to lean and depend on God. Often, in life, when things seemed to get hard, I learned I could always depend on and run to God, no matter how clouded the issue seemed. It took me a while to understand that, but now it is something I would never let go of. Yvonne showed me that when the world kicks me off, I could always run to God and that when I have God, I have all that I really need to stay afloat in the situation. She taught me that God in me was greater and bigger than any obstacles and any setbacks that I may experience in life. Oh, how these lessons have shaped me to be nothing like the child my parents left and rejected. If one could place the boy I was and the man I am side by side, they will find not one thing alike, I have grown that much. There are many things and events that happened to me that are unspoken of at this point in my life. There are some good things, and there are some bad things; bad habits that I had picked up and good habits that I picked up. Nevertheless, life is a learning lesson, and it's all a part of the process. Yvonne noticed that I had become a burden to everyone at this point, which was very hard for her to deal with. Comments were shared about helping and providing for me, but this did not stop her from providing for me. Yvonne worked at a middle school for several years and ran her own candy store, which was a major help.

There was this one time when we went to Tennessee to visit family; Matt was driving, and we were scheduled to stay for a few days. I got to meet a lot of family members that I never knew I had. The best part was they welcomed me with open arms. I never felt so much love from people who were related to me. The craziest part was I could run, yell, and scream all I wanted, and no one seemed to care. This was truly refreshing for me.

During this trip, I got to meet Yvonne's Husband, Jonny; I called him Papa Jonny. He was really glad to meet me; the feeling was mutual. The next day was July 4th, and the family drove a long way to see Yvonne. This was something big for the family as Yvonne was expecting more than 100 people for a cookout. One guy ran up and wrapped his arms around Yvonne's neck and said, "Aunt Yvonne! I am so glad to see you!" and she grabbed him and let him know she was glad to see him also. It was a great family reunion. My cousin Tamera was out there already, and a few family members asked about her whereabouts, but because of the issue that was going on with Cathy's husband, Kevin, and Yvonne falling out, they did not allow Tamera to travel with Yvonne this time. Many people remembered her from when she was smaller.

Chapter 8

I will always cherish the trip I took to Tennessee with Yvonne. Now, I am back at it since school has started back. It's time for third grade. I was placed on hyperactive medication with the hope it would help me focus better in class.

But with one positive came a negative; the bullying still would not go away. There were two twin boys that continued to bully and pick on me along with other kids. I complained to my grandmother and the bus driver about what was going on, but they just would not stop. On several occasions, the twins jumped me when I got on the bus. I ran home crying because I hated it more than anything that they just would not stop! The boy's dad came up to the bus stop and pushed the boys to fight me. Every day when getting off the bus, I took off running home.

Yvonne was sick and tired of being sick and tired of it all. She told me, "You better not come back crying and you better not run no more, or I am going to whoop you!" It was nothing like a whooping from Yvonne. When she sat in her chair, she had a long switch that reached from her chair to the door, and for anyone that got out of hand, she would get them back in place, which was enough. Hiding in her chair was "Big Willy," her gun. Grandma did not play and was not taking any junk from anyone. She always meant what she said.

The Bible says in Deuteronomy 31: 6 *'Be strong and of good courage, do not fear nor be afraid of them; for the LORD your God, He is the One who goes with you. He will not leave you nor forsake you'*, in Joshua 1: 9 *'Have I not commanded you? Be strong and of good courage; do not be afraid, nor be dismayed, for the LORD your God is with you wherever you go'*, and also in 2 Timothy 1: 7 *'For God has not given us a spirit of fear, but of power and of love and of a sound mind.'* With a firm hand, Yvonne taught me all of these. The twins were a threat to my peace and sanity, and not a lot of people usually understand how deep and intense bullying can go in the life of a young and growing child. When a child is constantly bullied, they will begin to look at themselves with the same eyes the bullies use to see them. Their self-confidence, self-esteem, self-love, and worth for themselves will go down the drain. They will see no value in themselves and sometimes, they even lose the will to live. None of these sound like what God wants for his own. He said in His word that he has not given us a spirit of fear but a spirit of a sound mind. A sound mind is free of doubts and confusion, and a sound mind is sure of the substance that has been put into him by God. Yvonne was sick of me running away; sometimes, you have got to look the devil in the face and let him know that the one who is in you is greater than the one in the world. That is what Yvonne forced me to learn at my early stage of life.

The next day, the twins were onto me again. I did not want them to get me, and I did not want Yvonne to get me either. I rushed off the school bus and began to run home as fast as I could. As I saw the gate, I approached it and saw Yvonne waiting at the door. I immediately stopped running and began to walk through the gate. Just as I passed the gate, the twins ran up behind me, and we began to fight.

But this time, I did not come to play. I readied my arms and began beating the twins with all the hatred and anger I held in. I am someone who never had the heart to hurt anything or anyone, the twins were receiving the payback they deserved. As if two weren't enough, their cousin arrived shortly after. Their aunt lived across the field and spotted the twins getting beat and sent help; however, that was never going to stop me.

"If he wants some, he can get it too," I stated to the twins. This went on until the three of them realized they would never win, and when they ran away, I knew I was the champion. But this was not the last of it; their dad was pissed off that the boys left running, so the next day, he and his wife were at the bus stop, and things began to heat up when the dad demanded a rematch. They also knew that because Yvonne was a big woman, was older, and was not able to make it to the bus stop, so the dad stopped me in my tracks. Not letting me leave, he made his boys fight me again. While in the middle of our rematch, Yvonne had the instinct that something was happening and called the police. Not only did Yvonne call the police, but she had Big Willy in one of her big pockets. She approached us and screamed, "Leave him alone!" The dad of the twins saw them coming and stopped the fight. When the police arrived, everyone went about their own business as if nothing had ever happened. This may seem like a lost fight, but rather, it was a great victory for me. A big win that would come in handy in me managing bully for the rest of my life. I was proud of myself, and I know Yvonne was too.

Several months later, things seemed to have quieted down. But within the family, grief struck us. Yvonne's oldest son, Jim, passed away unexpectedly. Everyone took his death hard, especially Yvonne. The family had not lost someone so close to them in a long time. Already separated, not only was Yvonne struggling with the dispute she was fighting with her daughter, Cathy, but now with the loss of Jim. Jim was the oldest of six children. He would often come and stay at Yvonne's and spend time with them. Many stated that Jim was gay, but he had a wife and stepdaughter, so they had no proof of this rumor. The family spoke with the doctor about Jim's death, and they did not provide many details other than that he was unresponsive when they found him.

When the day of the funeral arrived, Yvonne was not doing well. She could not stop crying and could barely walk. Everyone was at the church, and it was time to get lined up. I wanted to be by my grandmother's side, but everyone else was already surrounding her for support. I could not stand to see her hurt. I could see her pain, and I could not help but worry about her.

My dad and uncle Matt tried to get her out of the limo to go into the church, but they were having a hard time. The boys finally found a way to get her out of the limo and helped her inside.

As we walked down the aisles, I could hear Uncle Jim's wife and daughter scream and cry inside the church; they were taking Jim's passing extremely hard. My grandmother cried as she walked into the church. By that time, everyone was grieving.

I could not take it; all I wanted was to be with my grandmother to comfort her and tell her that everything was going to be okay, and that Uncle Jim was resting with the Lord, but they would not let me get close to her. When the service started, Matt slouched down, and escorts helped him outside. He and Jim were very close, and he was having a very hard time coping with everything that happened.

Chapter 9

Several months had passed, and I had worked very hard to make As and Bs in school. My teacher, Mrs. Small, worked hard to make sure I got what I needed, and I started to focus on my work. She was very proud of me as I continued to do well in class. Before school started back up for the New Year, I had a nice break from being bullied and picked on, which was a nice, temporary relief. But it was not too much longer until things would pick back up. One of my neighbors, Jontray, came and played with me from time to time. Over time, we became close friends. Jontraye stopped a lot of the kids from picking on me when he was around. He never cared for that kind of behavior. That year in school, there was a big trip coming up that the fourth grade would take to visit The White House. One of the church members, Dr. Gems, offered to pay for my trip. This was something that Yvonne could not afford. In fact, she spent her last remaining dollars to make sure I had the money I needed for food and things for school. This was also part of her bill money. One of the school parents, Mrs. Ward, reassured Yvonne that everything was going to be okay, and she would make sure I got everything I needed.

While on the trip, things back home really took off. Tamera fell sick, and they were not sure what was going on with her. Upon a check-up with a doctor, she found she was pregnant with Kevin's child. Everyone was heated and went off on Kevin. Yvonne tried her best to tell Cathy what was going on, which ended up splitting the family. But that did not stop her from what she wanted to believe. So, everything that Cathy was fighting Yvonne against finally came to light. She knew it was bound to happen sooner or later.

With the three of them living in the house and no one to stop him, what was being done in the dark will most definitely come to light. This was something that would devastate Tamera for life. But the saddest part was that no one would ever find out that he also took advantage of me as well because there was no way to prove it. You see, I did not matter, so no one thought to ask or even have me checked out. As time passed, the hurt my family was enduring did not cease. But some were able to let go of the pain and move on. Yvonne's friend, Maria, remained at her side during all of this. Maria sometimes came and helped Yvonne around the house and did what she could.

Janet and Cathy decided to take Yvonne and her children to Disney, and because of how Maria stepped in as a great friend to Yvonne, they decided to take her with them. They drove down, and everyone was excited for the fun trip ahead.

A few months later, Yvonne fell ill and had to be rushed to the hospital. They determined she suffered from a light heart attack and had to be hospitalized for several days. This was extremely hard for me to go through. While Yvonne was in the hospital, I had to stay next door with Janet. She would talk about how actions spoke louder than words because you could tell in that case that I was not really welcome. But in the meantime, Janet adjusted to making room for me while Yvonne was in the hospital.

Since being in the hospital, Yvonne improved and was stable enough to come home. The girls managed to get her in the house without me knowing. They wanted to let her get some rest because I continued to ask about Yvonne and how she was doing. Eventually, they allowed me to see her. Over the next few months, Yvonne regained her strength. At that point, Yvonne realized even more that she was all I truly had. This was a very hard pill to swallow, but she continued to not let anything stop her. The love that I received from Yvonne was very significant in my upbringing. Yvonne's love and care for me were unconditional and pure. She had every reason under heaven to not be so involved in my upbringing; an old greying woman with bills to cover and her health to be worried about, but she chose to care for me in a way I may have thought was normal, but I have now seen that it was intentional and very scarce. It was so pure that not everyone could afford it, especially not my parents.

It was the day before Christmas, and everyone was at Yvonne's house. For the past few years, I constantly asked to see my mother, but she let me down time and again. It was getting late in the evening, and I was ready to leave, but Yvonne wasn't. She had no issue putting me in my place. I got upset as a result. Eventually, Yvonne was ready, and I took off running across the field. Yvonne yelled out for me to come back and help her walk so she would not fall. Reluctantly, I came back and helped Yvonne walk across the field. Once we got back in the house, I headed toward my room, and guess who popped out of the closet and surprised me? My mother! This was the best Christmas gift I could have asked for. "Momma," I whispered in a soft voice, then began to run and wrap my arms around her, crying with tears of excitement. I had not seen her in several years. Yvonne had worked hard to do what she could to get Leyka there this holiday season. She fought tooth and nail and was able to make it happen. She was also filled with joy to see me happy, but all good things must come to an end. The visit would not last long, and when the day after Christmas arrived, Leyka disappeared again, and the visit became a simple memory.

A few months after Christmas, Yvonne finally allowed me to stay the night at Jontraye's house. Tyrone told her she could not keep me locked up all the time. You see, the local children in the neighborhood would often make jokes about me being on house arrest because Yvonne would not let me go anywhere. She loved me, and I knew it always, but I did not understand that her love for me was the only reason why she did some things and enforced some laws in my life. I wish I had trusted her judgment enough to be thoroughly satisfied with it. You see, that is the way it is with God and His children (you and I) a lot of times. God says to you, very clearly, He says 'oh, do not do that, or do not touch that' and you think 'this God must hate me to try to stop me from being 'happy' or having the kind of fun that I want to have so badly. We fail to see that if He says this, then it is definitely going to be for our own good. The Bible says in Proverbs 3:5 *'Trust in the* LORD *with all your heart and lean not on your own understanding; in all your ways acknowledge Him, and He shall direct your paths.'* This is what God wants us to do, because He loves us and wants only the best for us all the time. The moment we choose to rely on our own understanding, we say to God 'you know what? I think I've got this. You can let me have control of my life now,' and boy, that is chaotic! Yvonne knew what was best asking me to stay indoors but I did not like the idea of it, so when people started saying she should let me out, I was not oppositive at all.

We had been playing outside all night, and his mom asked us to come inside because it was getting dark. As we were watching a movie, I got sleepy, so they told me to go to the back room and lay down. As I walked back there, it was scary. I was the only one back there, but I soon fell asleep.

After sleeping for a while, I began to feel someone come and lay beside me. At first, I thought it was Jontraye. As I was lying there, I felt someone touch me, and I instantly jumped up and saw what was going on. Being half-asleep, I was lost and confused. It was Jontraye's brother, Dion. As soon as I jumped up, he told me to be quiet since everyone was asleep. I asked him, "Where is Jontraye?"

He said, "He fell asleep in the living room, but you are good. Just lay down and go back to sleep." I laid back down and dozed back off to sleep. After a while, I woke up again to someone touching me. This time, my pants were halfway down, and Dion was trying to slide himself inside of me. I instantly tried to jump away, but he held me down. I was so scared at that moment, and I was not sure what to do. He whispered in my ear, "Shhhh, do not say anything. I got you. It's okay." I began to cry as he continued to force himself inside of me. It began to hurt more and more the further he penetrated. He was lying on top of me, and I could not move. I was helpless, unable to defend myself. All I could do was just lay there and take it. After he finished, he told me in my ear that I better not tell anyone or else. Then, he lay beside me. At that point, I was not sure what to do or say. I just lay there until everyone in the house woke up. Once they were up, I went home instantly.

Once I got home, my grandmother said, "You are home early. Is everything okay?" I just looked at her and replied, "Yes," and went to my room and laid down. I was not sure if I should have said something or not; I just did not say anything at all. I simply kept it to myself.

Chapter 10

It's springtime, and one of the church members agreed to take me to breakfast by the ball field. This was something that I really enjoyed. Often times she altered my suits. I used to love to sit on the front row at church, as Yvonne made sure I was well dressed and ready every Sunday. A few weeks later, the family also received a major call that Alvina, Yvonne's mother, had passed away. Alvina was the name of Yvonne's and Harriet's mother. She had 4 children, Yvonne, Big Jim, who had passed away before I was born, Cara, who was the youngest of the four, and Harriet. But after phone calls were made, they found out it was the wrong Alvina; the phone call Harriet received was actually about my grandfather's mother. You see, Yvonne was also married to a man who was the father of Markus, Matt, Janet, and Tyrone. His mother's name was also Alvina. Shortly after we got this information, Harriet's health began to decline. This was not good for her to go back and forth to the doctor, as she seemed to be doing better.

A few months had passed, and while Yvonne was sitting in the living room, she got a call to go up to Harriet's immediately. She headed up to Harriet's and discovered she was not doing well. She was vomiting and choking, and they were unable to get it to stop. Yvonne called 911, and as they arrived, the paramedics were unable to get things in order. They rushed her to the nearest medical center where she worked, and all the family was called in. Yvonne and Cara did what they could to take care of their sister. They all stood in the waiting area at the hospital. When the doctor walked in, he let the family know that Harriet had suffered several seizures, and they were working hard to get them under control.

As the night passed over, things were still not looking good, and Harriet took a turn for the worst. They rushed her to a hospital about an hour away to get more care from someone who was more familiar with what was going on. While being transported to the next hospital, Harriet had several strokes, heart attacks, and seizures. The doctors were fighting to do what they could to keep her alive. A few weeks passed, and Harriet was still in the hospital, and at that point, they determined that Harriet had a rare type of colon cancer. Having this information, the doctors were doing what they could to take control of it, but it was not easy. Yvonne had to go back and forth to the hospital while trying to take care of me, which was putting a lot on her. But she was not giving up on her sister's health.

A few days passed, and my family heard the news they never wanted to hear; Harriet had passed away. Both sisters began to take it hard as this was not an easy pill for them to swallow. You see, Yvonne and Harriet were like two peas on a pod. Having lost a son a few years prior and now her sister, what more could she possibly take? As time passed, they had the funeral. Harriet's death was a hard pill for the family to get over but then would move forward with the grace of God.

Chapter 11

As the school year passed, I was doing very well in school, pushing myself to do what I could to get my schoolwork done. Yvonne fought to make sure I understood what was going on. One day, I forgot to take my medicine, and the school had to call Yvonne to tell her I was acting up. When Yvonne arrived at school, she requested that the teacher come down to meet her. Yvonne was very upset with me to learn I had been acting up, and they had to call her. This big woman did not come to play as the teacher walked into the office. Yvonne laid her eyes on me, which felt like daggers piercing my face. The next thing you knew, a loud "smack" went across my face. She did not care who saw her and who was around; she did not play around when one of her own was acting up in school. I was there to learn, and that's what she meant for me to do. I needed to take as much information in as I could to learn, not play, so she hit me so hard that it made the teacher cry. I straightened my act up and got it together before returning back to the classroom. Later that day, when I got home, Yvonne was still upset about having to leave work to go and deal with me. I knew it was going to be a rough night.

Yvonne always did what she had to do to bring out the lion in me. What she did may not always seem okay to the rest of the world, but it was necessary to train me right and bring me up in the way a great man should be brought up. If she had let me loose, allowed me to act silly, spend nights out of the house, or be irresponsible, no good would have come of me. She was ready to do what it took and that is what brought me thus far in my journey in life. Greatness is not going to just appear in the life of a person, it will have to be bred, watched, and nurtured from a little age. Let us look at the story of the life of David for example. 1 Samuel 17 reads:

Now the Philistines gathered their armies together to battle, and were gathered at Sochoh, which belongs to Judah; they encamped between Sochoh and Azekah, in Ephes Dammim. And Saul and the men of Israel were gathered together, and they encamped in the Valley of Elah, and drew up in battle array against the Philistines. The Philistines stood on a mountain on one side, and Israel stood on a mountain on the other side, with a valley between them.

And a champion went out from the camp of the Philistines, named Goliath, from Gath, whose height was six cubits and a span. He had a bronze helmet on his head, and he was armed with a coat of mail, and the weight of the coat was five thousand shekels of bronze. And he had bronze armor on his legs and a bronze javelin between his shoulders. Now the staff of his spear was like a weaver's beam, and his iron spearhead weighed six hundred shekels; and a shield-bearer went before him. Then he stood and cried out to the armies of Israel, and said to them, "Why have you come out to line up for battle? Am I not a Philistine, and you the servants of Saul? Choose a man for yourselves and let him come down to me. If he is able to fight with me and kill me, then we will be your servants. But if I prevail against him and kill him, then you shall be our servants and serve us." And the Philistine said, "I defy the armies of Israel this day; give me a man, that we may fight together." When Saul and all Israel heard these words of the Philistine, they were dismayed and greatly afraid.

Now David was the son of that Ephrathite of Bethlehem Judah, whose name was Jesse, and who had eight sons. And the man was old, advanced in years, in the days of Saul. The three oldest sons of Jesse had gone to follow Saul to the battle. The names of his three sons who went to the battle were Eliab the firstborn, next to him Abinadab, and the third Shammah. David was the youngest. And the three oldest followed Saul. But David occasionally went and returned from Saul to feed his father's sheep at Bethlehem.

And the Philistine drew near and presented himself forty days, morning and evening.

Then Jesse said to his son David, "Take now for your brothers an ephah of this dried grain and these ten loaves and run to your brothers at the camp. And carry these ten cheeses to the captain of their thousand, and see how your brothers fare, and bring back news of them." Now Saul and they and all the men of Israel were in the Valley of Elah, fighting with the Philistines.

So, David rose early in the morning, left the sheep with a keeper, and took the things and went as Jesse had commanded him. And he came to the camp as the army was going out to the fight and shouting for the battle. For Israel and the Philistines had drawn up in battle array, army against army. And David left his supplies in the hand of the supply keeper, ran to the army, and came and greeted his brothers. Then as he talked with them, there was the champion, the Philistine of Gath, Goliath by name, coming up from the armies of the Philistines; and he spoke according to the same words. So, David heard them. And all the men of Israel, when they saw the man, fled from him and were dreadfully afraid. So, the men of Israel said, "Have you seen this man who has come up? Surely, he has come up to defy Israel; and it shall be that the man who kills him the king will enrich with great riches, will give him his daughter, and give his father's house exemption from taxes in Israel."

Then David spoke to the men who stood by him, saying, "What shall be done for the man who kills this Philistine and takes away the reproach from Israel? For whom is this uncircumcised Philistine, that he should defy the armies of the living God?"

And the people answered him in this manner, saying, "So shall it be done for the man who kills him."

Now Eliab his oldest brother heard when he spoke to the men; and Eliab's anger was aroused against David, and he said, "Why did you come down here? And with whom have you left those few sheep in the wilderness? I know your pride and the insolence of your heart, for you have come down to see the battle."

And David said, "What have I done now? Is there not a cause?" Then he turned from him toward another and said the same thing; and these people answered him as the first ones did.

Now when the words which David spoke were heard, they reported them to Saul; and he sent for him. Then David said to Saul, "Let no man's heart fail because of him; your servant will go and fight with this Philistine."

And Saul said to David, "You are not able to go against this Philistine to fight with him; for you are a youth, and he a man of war from his youth."

But David said to Saul, "Your servant used to keep his father's sheep, and when a lion or a bear came and took a lamb out of the flock, I went out after it and struck it, and delivered the lamb from its mouth; and when it arose against me, I caught it by its beard, and struck and killed it. Your servant has killed both lion and bear; and this uncircumcised Philistine will be like one of them, seeing he has defied the armies of the living God." Moreover, David said, "The Lord, who delivered me from the paw of the lion and from the paw of the bear, He will deliver me from the hand of this Philistine."

And Saul said to David, "Go, and the Lord be with you!"

So, Saul clothed David with his armor, and he put a bronze helmet on his head; he also clothed him with a coat of mail. David fastened his sword to his armor and tried to walk, for he had not tested them. And David said to Saul, "I cannot walk with these, for I have not tested them." So, David took them off.

Then he took his staff in his hand; and he chose for himself five smooth stones from the brook, and put them in a shepherd's bag, in a pouch which he had, and his sling was in his hand. And he drew near to the Philistine. So, the Philistine came, and began drawing near to David, and the man who bore the shield went before him. And when the Philistine looked about and saw David, he disdained him; for he was only a youth, ruddy and good-looking. So, the Philistine said to David, "Am I a dog, that you come to me with sticks?" And the Philistine cursed David by his gods. And the Philistine said to David, "Come to me, and I will give your flesh to the birds of the air and the beasts of the field!"

Then David said to the Philistine, "You come to me with a sword, with a spear, and with a javelin. But I come to you in the name of the Lord of hosts, the God of the armies of Israel, whom you have defied. This day the Lord will deliver you into my hand, and I will strike you and take your head from you. And this day I will give the carcasses of the camp of the Philistines to the birds of the air and the wild beasts of the earth, that all the earth may know that there is a God in Israel. Then all this assembly shall know that the Lord does not save with sword and spear; for the battle is the Lord's, and He will give you into our hands."

So it was, when the Philistine arose and came and drew near to meet David, that David hurried and ran toward the army to meet the Philistine. Then David put his hand in his bag and took out a stone; and he slung it and struck the Philistine in his forehead, so that the stone sank into his forehead, and he fell on his face to the earth. So, David prevailed over the Philistine with a sling and a stone and struck the Philistine and killed him. But there was no sword in the hand of David. Therefore, David ran and stood over the Philistine, took his sword and drew it out of its sheath and killed him, and cut off his head with it.

And when the Philistines saw that their champion was dead, they fled. Now the men of Israel and Judah arose and shouted and pursued the Philistines as far as the entrance of the valley and to the gates of Ekron. And the wounded of the Philistines fell along the road to Shaaraim, even as far as Gath and Ekron. Then the children of Israel returned from chasing the Philistines, and they plundered their tents. And David took the head of the Philistine and brought it to Jerusalem, but he put his armor in his tent.

When Saul saw David going out against the Philistine, he said to Abner, the commander of the army, "Abner, whose son is this youth?"

And Abner said, "As your soul lives, O king, I do not know." So, the king said, "Inquire whose son this young man is."

Then, as David returned from the slaughter of the Philistine, Abner took him and brought him before Saul with the head of the Philistine in his hand. And Saul said to him, "Whose son are you, young man?"

So, David answered, "I am the son of your servant Jesse the Bethlehemite.'

What have you been able to pick from this highlight in the life of David? I will tell you what I picked; everything the Lord brings your way is to prepare you for your life of glory and greatness. Every experience, every obstacle, every duty, and every responsibility, all of it will make you ready and bring you closer to the life of greatness God is preserving for you. David was left to take care of his father's sheep while his brothers had the advantage of going out to the city. He was like an errand boy, taking food to them, caring for the sheep all day long but what did he do? He accepted all of these with diligence. David worked hard and put his heart into a job that may have been taken lightly by others. We were made to know that even if it were one of his father's sheep that was attacked by a bear or a lion, David would go after it. Such diligence! All of it prepare him for a day he did not know would come, a day that made him known throughout his city.

In the same light, God prepares you and me with little experiences here and there and you must not take it as a punishment. It is meant to push you forward and further into the grand plan that He has for your life of greatness.

Chapter 12

After winter break, it was time to get back into the swing of things. But this time, there was an issue with the teachers. I went into my first class, and things started off rocky. There was a new topic we learned, and I approached my teacher for help so I could understand it better.

"Excuse me, but could you explain this to me again?"

"No, go read the book and take notes." She responded, refusing to look at my notes or even acknowledge my presence.

When I went home, I told my grandmother what had happened, and she told me to go to school. My grandmother told my dad to go to the school and see what was going on. She was not able to go so she asked my dad to go. My dad walked in the school without stopping by the office and checking in. She came and found me and watched the teacher do me wrong. He called her out and she told him right away that he needed to go to the office. When he went to the office and talked to the principal, but he sided with the teacher. In reality, the teacher was refusing to help me by giving me pushback. Every time I gave the teacher my notes, she threw them away, disregarding them completely. Even my classmates noticed what was going on.

Shocked by this, I responded, "What are you talking about?! I am getting my work done, and I just wanted her to explain something to me." The principal was not having it and sided with the teacher regardless.

That resulted in me being held back in the sixth grade. Having to deal with something like this with a teacher was not normal, as I normally had great relationships with my teachers. For the first time, I had a teacher who did not like me. But this year, there was nothing but one issue after the other, and somehow it was always my fault. But it was whatever at that point because I was the kid and the teacher was in charge, and because of that prejudice, they knew what was best.

When summer finally arrived, it was time for me to go and enjoy the outside feel, but grandma would not let me, which I did not understand. Rather than letting me go outside and spend time with friends, she made me stay inside to bake a cake with her. Although I missed being outside, I did enjoy the quality time we spent together baking cakes.

One day, I wanted to play outside, but she made me grab her ice water. But I did not listen. She did not let me go outside and have fun, so she did not deserve her nightly ice water. She needed her ice water, but I was being stubborn. Suddenly, I heard her calling for me, "Sidney, will you come in here please?" I went into her room, and she mentioned she wanted to have a heart-to-heart. "You know, there will be no one who will treat you the same once I am gone." I looked at her, silent.

"They do not care about you like I care." She explained that everything that I received and everything that happened was because she made it happen. She continued, "I fought to make sure you had everything you needed." She told me that I needed to learn all I could from her since she won't always be there in the future.

Tears began to flow down my cheek, "I.... I do not understand. What's going on?" Not even thinking, I ran into my room, grabbed markers and a piece of paper, and drew a picture of Yvonne and me together. I returned to her room, gave her the picture, and said, "I wanted to tell you I love you."

"I love you too." She spoke.

Since grandma raised me, I was like the baby brother to six children she already had. The rest of the siblings had to step in and help raise me, but they hated it and wanted nothing to do with me. Truth be told, they felt I was the reason for her health issues. Janet stepped in and did all she could to help me, but she gained resentment against me. Her actions spoke more loudly than her words. You could tell I was not welcome around. She and Traci would make comments about me. Janet always stayed next door to Yvonne and me, so whenever she needed help with something, Janet was there to help. What came to pass was Traci was jealous of the attention Yvonne gave me.

One thing was for sure, grandma and I cooked and baked together so she could show me what she knew. That summer, I visited Lenoir and spent time with my Uncle Craig and his family. Uncle Craig had a large farm with chickens, and I loved to chase them in the yard, but then they would figure out what was happening and chase me back to the house. Even when one of the chickens grabbed me, they could never get a hold of me, so I did not care. It was still fun.

Chapter 13

I could not believe it; this was the year I was going to be a teenager. My 13th birthday. I was so excited about this exciting milestone, and all I could think of was how much I wanted a bike. But Yvonne told me that getting a bike was not possible, and I had no choice but to move on; however, I refused to listen and did not stop asking.

On Thursday morning, August 27, 1998, Yvonne came into my room and woke me up for school. To begin with, I was not in a good mood after finding out I was not getting the one thing I wanted for my birthday, so I dragged my feet to get ready for school. I wanted anything and everything but to go to school that day.

"Get up and get ready now!" she fussed at me. I did not care and continued to throw a fit, but what I did not realize was there a surprise waiting for me in the living room. As soon as I turned the corner into the living room, a beautiful burgundy bike was sitting in the center of the room. I could not believe my eyes. The one thing I wanted for my birthday was sitting within reach of me, and ever after Yvonne said she was not getting me one, there it was! I could not wait to come home from school and ride it. I turned around and ran to Yvonne to give her the biggest hug, "Thank you, thank you, thank you Grandma!"

"You are welcome, Sidney." She replied, hugging me back. It was the best start to my birthday I could ask for. After celebrating, reality kicked back in as I was restarting the sixth grade again. Even though I faced this setback, I did not let it affect my school year, and thankfully, I did not face many problems this time around. I hoped that this year was going to be better. My school put different things into place that helped me more than last year, and it was a blessing.

But then the day came when Yvonne decided that it was her time to leave. For months, she had been talking about leaving for Tennessee and set a date to leave on February 7, 1999. I was always with Yvonne, but this time she was taking this trip on her own, and I had to stay next door with Janet for two weeks. I was never thrilled to spend time over there. Although Janet never said anything negative to me, her actions said otherwise. But there was nothing I could do; she bought her ticket and took off. A week after Yvonne left, she made sure to call me multiple times to check on me. One day, she called and asked Janet to speak to me. I was upset since I was somewhere I did not want to be, but I took the phone.

"Hey, grandma," I said with a dry tone.

"How are you doing?" She asked me.

"I am fine. When are you coming home?"

"I will be home soon. I love you."

"I love you too." I ended the call.

Later that night, Janet received a phone call that Yvonne had become unresponsive after eating dinner. It took the ambulance more than 30 minutes to an hour to get there because of where the house was located. Unfortunately, when they arrived, it was too late. I remember sitting in the living room when Janet received the call. She approached me and told me that grandma was not well, and they called an ambulance. I went into another room and started to cry, unaware of what was to come next. I could not even stand knowing my grandmother, the woman who raised me, was not doing well, and there was nothing I could do to help her. Tossing and turning, I went back into the kitchen and saw Janet on the phone, crying. I asked her, "How is she doing? Is she okay?"

Janet slowly turned to face me, and her face said it all. Her eyes were red and blotchy. She said, "Bernard, I told you, mama's gone." That's when I completely lost it.

I refused to hear the words that just came out of her mouth. "What did you just say?"

"She's gone." Janet repeated.

I completely lost it. My world, my everything, my Yvonne, was gone. The one and the only person who cared about me was gone in an instant. I was just on the phone with her saying I love you, not even knowing that was going to be the last time I heard her voice. My heart shattered into a million pieces that night. Janet and Traci did everything they could to help me calm down, but nothing worked. I was inconsolable.

Janet reached out to Gina, Rita's daughter, to try and help me calm down. Once they calmed me down, I was panting and could barely breathe. Gina came over to hold me, hugged me tight, and told me to breathe with her. But I could barely breathe. My entire world was rocked and blown into oblivion, and every thought, feeling, and every item I saw was a blurry mess. Gina held onto me tightly and rocked me to try and provide comfort, "Everything is going to be okay." My heart was racing, and I began to hyperventilate. "Breath with me," she said as she started breathing to help my body relax. After a while, it finally worked, and I was able to gather myself, but it was not easy.

Cathy was also having trouble calming down Tamera as well. Everyone was distraught; our matriarch was gone. While Gina was with me, Janet was in the kitchen trying to get a hold of Tyrone, but he was working the third shift and was hard to get in touch with. She told him that he needed to come immediately to check on me.

Later, Tyrone arrived and saw Gina holding me tightly. As soon as he stepped through the door, he headed toward me, thinking I was acting out. Before he reached me, Janet stopped him in his tracks. "Mama just died." In great disbelief, Tyrone fell back into the sofa and cried out. No one in the family knew what to say, how to think, or how to feel. This death was so unexpected, and we loved Yvonne more than anything in this world. We did not know what was going to happen with the family now with her gone forever. That night, Tyrone took me down to Reba to stay with her for the night. I was completely heartbroken by the news but somehow, I chose to remember

Yvonne's teachings. I thought about the part of the Bible in Romans 8:28 that *says, 'And we know that all things work together for good to those who love God, to those who are the called according to His purpose'* and I chose to trust that this too, was planned by God for a greater will and purpose. It did not make any sense to me that Yvonne had to die and leave me all alone in the sad cold world, but I chose to think of the plan of God, and slowly but eventually, I made peace with it.

When everyone began planning Yvonne's funeral, I chipped in to make sure they knew what her request was: to be buried on a Sunday. I told them she also asked to have her funeral at Bright Star Church while wearing a white and dark gray dress she had hanging in her closet and only worn once. The family made sure to do everything they could to make sure Yvonne's requests were fulfilled, but this was nearly impossible for everyone to deal with.

As the days passed, reality began to really sink in. Yvonne's children spoke with the funeral director and were standing by Janet's front door. Then, I broke the silence. "Who am I going to stay with now?"

Then, Janet stepped in. "There is no room for him over here. My house is full, and we do not want to let him go to social service. Mamma would've had a fit."

Cathy added, "I have already raised my child. I am not raising anymore."

Matt chimed in, "He can come down here with the girls, but ain't nobody going to be bringing him back and forth up the road to that church." Everyone knew that Yvonne would've turned over in her grave if I was taken out of that church. Markus was also standing there, recently home from prison for the funeral, and had to go back once everything was done. The only person who was left was Tyrone.

"Well, I guess I will take him. He's my son." Then that was it; Dad and I were to stay in grandma's old apartment. Over the next few days, Tyrone and Reba argued about having me stay with them at their house. Since I was already living in grandma's apartment, everything was already in place, so Tyrone was allowed to move in and take everything from there. That left my dad and me a place to stay.

As the day of the funeral came closer, many friends and family members came to check up on us. Even people in the community came by to see how we were doing. When the day of the funeral arrived, I did not have it. I wished for the day to pass as quickly as it was to sneeze but having friends and church members visit built me up. The service ended up beautiful, and I will cherish it forever.

Afterward, Tyrone and Reba sat outside in the car in front of the church while the family ate inside. I went out to the car to check on them and found Reba pissed about how Chanda was there, as well as pissed at me for some reason. Reba looked my way and demanded that I leave her car immediately.

Tyrone interjected, "Do not be like that!" He looked at me and told me to leave her car. To prevent that issue from escalating, I left the car and went back inside to join the family. By this time, the other fire began to boil. Matt was upset that Cathy did not come to Yvonne's funeral due to her being a

Jehovah's Witness. They did not believe in going to church, but Cathy allowed Tamera to go to the fellowship hall to eat with the family.

As time passed, Tyrone and I stayed in grandma's old apartment. He also spent time hopping between staying with Reba and the apartment with me. He was trying to make things work, trying to force something that Reba did not want. Over time she moved closer to where the apartment was, not to make his life easier, but because she had no choice. Since I was not her child, Reba wanted nothing to do with me.

Over the next few weeks, my dad leaned more toward leaving me alone so I would fend for myself in the apartment. I would not even see him for days at a time. There were times I had to go to the neighbors to work and get food since there was none in the apartment. He left me to fend for myself, a thirteen-year-old boy. Once Janet's husband, Victor, got out of prison, he stayed with us too. I saw different faces running in and out of the apartment daily. When I got myself ready for school every morning, I woke up my dad for work. He never stayed at the apartment with me but across the field where Reba lived. I would have to walk across the field, which was almost half a mile, give or take, to wake him up for work every morning. It was more as if I was the parent, and my dad was the child.

There was one night when Victor and I were home alone. Sometimes he walked around the house in his boxers alone. That specific night, we watched a movie, and he asked me, "What did you want to watch next?" We were in grandma's room on her old bed, which was my favorite place to watch movies with her. My grandma had a large amount of VHS tapes, and we would pick one together for movie night. "Pick a movie," he told me. I selected a random one that was around the corner Victor put it into the video player and pressed play; that's when I realized I accidentally selected a porno.

See, the Bible says in 1 Peter 5:8 *'Be sober, be vigilant; because your adversary the devil walks about like a roaring lion, seeking whom he may devour.'* The devil will never stop trying to pull you down, you need to know that and keep it at the top of your mind. The devil will do all that he can to beat you up and pull you down, but you should not allow him. When you have done a lot of work moving ahead, the devil comes with his praying eyes and tries to bring you back to zero. No matter what, you should always get back up.

I immediately jumped up and headed to the TV to turn it off, but Victor beat me to it. "It's okay, keep it on. You can watch it." Reluctantly, I stayed put and watched it with him. Victor erected himself and began to pleasure himself. I had no idea what to do in this situation; I just sat there. Then, he turned to me and asked me to take off my pants

My grandmother always kept Vaseline on her old waterbed. The headboard had a mirror in the center with shelves on either side of the headboard.

He rolled me onto my stomach, he tried to slide himself into my rear but was not successful. He grabbed more Vaseline; he held me down and forced himself into me. He found his way into me, but all I could feel was horrible pain and stretch from him. After he had seen that I was in a lot of pain, he pulled out and told me to not tell anyone. I got up in pains; I was bleeding. Still in pain, I fell asleep, physically and emotionally drained. I missed my grandma more than ever.

Then, things began to get harder. Different utility bills began to tally up and, with no one paying, resulted in them being shut off. First, it was the water, then the lights. Rather than stepping in to be a father and a good man who took care of his son, he chose to devote his time, money, and attention to the woman across the field. Tyrone was still running between Reba's house and the apartment and never cared to take a second look at what was happening to me. Seeing no food in the apartment was a normal thing to see, from what little I was able to see with the lights shut off.

Ms. Sadie often allowed me to come and help her do things around the house in exchange for a delicious meal. She knew my situation and would often offer me food, so I stayed fed. Although she did not have much, she did everything she could to provide for me. She was not the only one who picked up what was happening behind closed doors. It got to the point where social services were called, but Tyrone quickly fixed any problem to close the case. I was stuck with nothing to do and nowhere to go.

When summer came, things got worse. The neighbor's boys began to hang out at my house. With no adults around, it was bound that anything and everything could and would happen.

Chapter 14

This year left surprises that I never thought would come to pass. My dad convinced Reba to let me come over there, knowing she would never let me stay. One day when we were sitting around the house, there was a knock at the door. Reba opened the door, and there stood the police with a warrant for my dad's arrest. "We have a warrant for Tyrone's arrest." I did not know what to think. It was found that he was behind in his child support for Reba's child, and she had called the police on him. This was a betrayal. What made no sense was the child had been living there with them this entire time, so to claim he never paid for child support was stupid and crazy. There was nothing I could do to stop it. The only thing I could do was run back to the apartment with tears in my eyes, knowing that we would have to leave grandma's apartment forever since he had stopped paying for rent.

It was now time for school to start, and the landlord evicted my dad and me since he had fallen too far behind on his rent. The landlord did not want to put us out because of the relationship he had with grandma since she stayed for many years, but he had no choice. I had to leave the place where I grew up. The search began for a new place to live. My dad contacted my mom, and she sent some money for school cloths, which my dad took and spent on other things, only buying a shirt and some pants for school. The lights and water soon after got cut off in the apartment.

As time grew closer to our move-out date, dad still went back and forth between the apartment and Reba's. The realization hit me that I would have nowhere to go at 14 years old. I slept in a silver parked car in the back of my Cousin Kurt's house because when we were out, we were sent out of the apartment so we both had to go stay with Kurt at his house. I could not attend school, either, because I had no way to get there. With everything going on, I had already missed two weeks of school and was falling behind. It sank in for me that the love grandma gave me would not be received from anyone else.

After several weeks of being out of school, dad's sister, Cathy, offered to let me stay with her until my dad got back on his feet. Being that she was a Jehovah's Witness, she made me attend their meetings at church on Monday nights. She was not going to put any effort into taking me to church and choir rehearsal. At the same time, Cathy was preparing for her wedding to a family friend, Charley.

As the family prepared for the wedding, I heard Cathy and Janet talk about how Tamera worked for one of the local banks and opened an account for Janet's daughter for her future schooling. I asked them if they would do the same thing for me, but I was immediately turned down. Instead of even considering it, the subject instantly changed. I continued to attend meetings that Cathy required of me. Charley' son moved in with us, and Cathy made me share the sofa bed with him. This happened for the next several months.

One night, Charley's son stayed at the house. He was sleeping in the den on the other side of the house. Everyone was in bed sleeping, and all of a sudden, I heard movement in the hallway. I got up to see what was going on, and as I tip-toed down the hallway, I noticed that Charley' son was in Tamera's room leaning over her. I snuck back to the living room and laid back down, hoping he did not see or hear me. Over the next few days, I went back and forth on if I should tell Cathy or not.

The next day, Cathy and I were alone, and I finally saw an opportunity to tell Cathy what was going on. I told her what I saw about Charley's son hovering over Tamera. She instantly got enraged at me and told me, "You have no idea what you are talking about! Stay in your place, and there is nothing like that happening in my house."

I gave up and just moved on. A few days passed, and I noticed that Cathy did not say anything about what I said to anyone. A week later, I woke up and started getting ready for school. Then, something jumped off the deep end. Cathy came in and said, "Charley' son can't stay here anymore." She had come to find out sometime earlier that morning; Cathy went to the restroom and found out there was something going on. Then things fired up. She was crying and walking back and forth. For the first time ever, she called out of work; she never calls out of work. She also drove me to school instead of letting me catch the bus.

While driving me to school, she said, "I am sorry for not believing you." This was a pivotal moment for us. Over the next few weeks and months, Stacey moved out, and I eventually received word that my dad was coming to get me and move me back in with him. I begged Cathy not to let me go, but she told me that being with her was only temporary, and I had to go back to being with my dad.

Chapter 15

My dad came to pick me up, and I wished for nothing more than for him to simply act right as my dad, but there was nothing I could do about what was to come next. He was able to get a new home for us on Section 8, roughly 25 minutes from where I was living with Cathy. After settling in, Reba moved in shortly after. I had no feeling as to how I was supposed to feel about this new living situation. What pissed me off was how she came in and started chanting how things were going to be run.

Over the next few months, things at home became rocky. I did not have a way to get to church anymore, but that never kept me from wanting to be there. Some of the church members came to pick me up and take me whenever they could. Dad was supposed to take me to school, but he did not want to do this without me paying him, causing me to miss the first few days. He wanted me to pay him to take me to school. I had missed a few days of school, but it was not too bad to make me fall out. Then, there were times when there was nothing to drink at the house but beer.

"Is there anything to drink?" I asked him.

He went to the fridge, pulled out one of his beers, and handed it to me, "Drink it." Then he left. Reba and my sister, Yazmen, would go out for food but never bring me back anything. This was my new normal. Then, my dad's relationship with Reba remained as it was, full of fights, screaming matches, and whatever else you would see in a toxic relationship. This happened for many months.

That night, my dad cooked pig's feet with greens and cornbread. He also bought orange soda and coke for us to drink. When Reba finished packing her things to move out, she unloaded everything out of the house, and I could tell my dad was upset about what was going on. To try fixing the aura in the room, I got up to fix my plate. He walked in the kitchen as I was fixing my plate of food and started looking at the food and drinks, he then stopped me. "Do not eat that." He lifted the plate and smelled the food, then noticed that the drinks were opened. Suddenly, he realized that Reba had bleached everything. The one my dad kept as his partner; she was trying to take me out. "Do not eat that. I will go get you something." Since I always loved Mickey D's, he went to get my favorite meal: A double cheeseburger, fries, and a high c with no ice.

A while after Reba moved to High Point, Dad worked to try mending the broken bridge between them. Then, the same routine happened again, where I was left alone for days on end since they reconciled. But thankfully, I was never alone. The benefit of Bright Star Church was that it was one of the largest churches in the area, and members lived all over the city. Luckily for me, one of the church members lived a few houses down from where our home was.

This neighbor already knew the situation from before. She helped by feeding me when she had extra food. She also offered to take me to church every Sunday. I felt like I could not catch a break from what was happening in my life. Not only was I dealing with the crap at home, but the bullies started up their act again at school, talking about me and continuing to prevent me from enjoying school. It got to the point where I did not even want to go anymore. In addition to the school bullies, Danielle, my half-sister, Li Mia, and our cousin, Traci, would walk around the building and claim that I was not their brother or cousin. I did not understand why everyone hated me so much. What did I ever do to deserve this? This was something I would never forget but I was strong enough to let go of it all and forge ahead.

Chapter 16

This year, I had no choice but to go to the Hickory High School district, even though I lived in the Saint Stevens school district. This year was supposed to be 'sweet', but when I went to dad to ask if I could switch schools, he refused. I was stuck in a rut since he was still traveling back and forth between Hickory and High Point. School started again, and I worked over the summer doing little side jobs in the neighborhood to make money.

When I asked dad to take me to school, I basically had to pay him with the money I earned so he could buy beer; otherwise, he would not take me. Whatever happened to letting me live my life and keeping what is owed to me? Yeah, that did not exist here. If I did not pay him, he would not take me to school. I wished nothing more than to have another option, but I had reached a dead end. I had no choice, and not only was my money taken from me, but dad told me we were leaving. Apparently, Reba reported to Section 8 that she had been staying there, which canceled dad's Section 8 rights. Once again, I was left without food or any basic things I needed to live by. The landlord was kind and let him stay, but since dad never paid rent there, we were evicted, again. I missed grandma more than ever.

Thankfully, Kurt, dad's cousin, let us stay with him for a few weeks. This was the second time we had to move in with him. We moved back to the area where all of this started. I slept on the couch, and dad slept in the back room; this was home. But when we take one step forward, there comes two steps back. Dad's alcohol problem grew to a whole new level. He was also known as one of the neighborhood mechanics.

One day he was working on someone's car in Hickory, so we had to go back and forth from there to work on it. While there, sometimes, we picked up my cousin at Shelby so he could hang out with us for the weekend. When we were on the way back, I hopped into the front seat, Kurt in the back, and Tyrone in the driver's seat. We made it down from Shelby to Hickory in less than an hour; he sped his way down all the way, and I was terrified he was going to crash the car with us in it. When we were on the way home, I noticed that the more he drank, the faster the car went. It got to the point where I was so scared, I did not know what to do to make him slow down. He would not listen to me; he just did not think it was so serious.

"Please, slow down!" I pleaded to him. But he did not listen; the more I begged him and asked him to slow down, the faster he went. By this time, I held onto the door handle for dear life, hoping this was not going to end badly for all of us. When we reached and tried to go up the hill in Eastridge to drive through Ridgeview, the car went so fast that it jumped the hill. Then we went flying in the air, and the car was out of control. Kurt screamed in the back, demanding for him to slow down, "Stop it! You are going to kill us!" Suddenly, the car jumped and slammed into the curb and came to an abrupt stop.

I opened my eyes and saw that the car was one part on the road and one part on the sidewalk. My dad and I locked eyes and did not say a word. I broke my gaze, looked to the right, and saw there was a large tree sitting against the right of my door. I could not open my door; no matter what I did, it would not budge because it was that close, not even up to an inch. That was when I realized how reckless my dad was about everything and anything he came across. He did not care about my safety or my well-being. It was just fun and games to him. We came so close to hitting this tree on my side, that I would have been impaled or killed. I could not even get out but had to climb over the seat and out the back door to be safe again. Kurt and I did not know what to say but stood there in complete shock.

"Get back in the car." We refused to get back into the car with him after we almost died. The car was in shambles, barely able to drive away. Kurt was so upset about what just happened, so he and I walked the rest of the way back. We did not get back until three in the morning. It was one of the most terrifying moments in my life. Kurt was able to ride with him again, but it took everything in me not to ride with him again.

Over the next few weeks, my school continued onward, but something was different. Leyka would normally do everything she could to avoid communication with me. She had sent me money to shop for school clothes and items I needed for class. But, of course, dad stepped in and took the money for himself, leaving me with only a pair of jeans and one shirt to use for the entire school year. The Pastor of Bright Star Church became very close with Yvonne and me. He would reach out to me to see what I needed for school and never failed to be there for me.

But I remained confident and courageous and told him that I did not need anything. He knew I was lying to him. He looked at me and knew what I was wearing was not the clothes that I should be wearing to school.

"I am going to take you to get some clothes, proper clothes." The pastor told me. I did not have a response, only a smile full of gratitude. No one had ever done this for me before, other than Yvonne. Someone truly cared about my well-being, and it meant so much to me.

I had my people, and so did my dad. A group of men loved him as he was like one of their brothers. They all knew each other for years and let their children hang out and play with each other. Shane, one of the brothers, saw what was going on with dad and Reba and let me stay with them at their house. It was nice because I became best friends with Shane's son. With no surprise, dad leaves me again. It was like I was back to fend for myself again, with no food, stepping into the shoes of the parent and my dad as the child. But God never gave up on me. As I said, rejection had been a norm for me from a very young age, and even till this age and beyond, I continued to experience it; it almost became a regular thing. I am grateful for the times that I was abandoned because those tough times made me the man that I am today. They made me stand up for myself and take responsibility. Who knows what kind of a person I would be by now if I was spoon-fed and never allowed to be in charge of my well-being? Truth be told, God took care of me in ways I did not expect or even fathom. The Word of God in Matthew 6:25-32 *'Therefore I say to you, do not worry about your life, what you will eat or what you will drink; nor about your body, what you will put on. Is not life more than food and the body more than clothing? Look at the birds of the air, for they neither sow nor reap nor gather into barns; yet your heavenly Father feeds them. Are you not of more value than they? Which of you by worrying can add one cubit to his stature? "So why do you worry about clothing? Consider the lilies of the field, how they grow: they neither toil nor spin; and yet I say to you that even Solomon in all his glory was not arrayed like one of these. Now if God so clothes the grass of the field, which today is, and tomorrow is thrown into the oven, will He not much more clothe you, O you of little faith? "Therefore, do not worry, saying, 'What shall we eat?' or 'What shall we drink?' or 'What shall we wear?' For after all these things the Gentiles seek. For your heavenly Father knows that you need all these things.'* God showed me His face and made sure that I did not lack. He gave me the gift of job opportunities and the gift of church members and family friends that showed me care and took my needs as a priority.

No matter how long dad was gone in High Point, I felt safe at Shane's house. I was a part of a group where the group of kids went to the same high school and enjoyed similar hobbies. I believed I had found a safe space. After a few weeks passed, Shane's family took a trip to the local Food Maze for groceries. I always did whatever it took to make money. Previous jobs included mowing neighbors' lawns and building dog houses, then selling them for a profit. No matter the task or how hard it was, I was able to do it. While at Food Lion, I went up to the customer service desk and asked, "Excuse me, how old do you have to be to work here?"

"15 years old." The manager answered. This was awesome news! Since I turned 16 just a few months before, I was eligible for a job here. Excited, I asked for a job application. The best part? Shane's son and I received jobs! I could not have been more excited about this new adventure. When Shane found out we received jobs, he was so excited for us. I wish I knew what this feeling was like in my family. When we first started the job, Shane and his wife had given us a great time while we were at it. Every time we needed Shane to take us to work, he charged us gas money in exchange for transportation. I did not mind it. I had a decent place to lay my head and eat once more.

I was so happy with how my life was going. I was finally doing well in school and was thriving at my job. But, of course, there were challenges. A few times, Shane threatened to put me out if I did not give up my entire check for his personal expenses. I was having flashbacks to how my dad would use my hard-earned money for beer. But I did not fight Shane because I could not afford to be without a home again. The house they were living in was small and was getting to the point where there was not much room for everyone anymore. So, we moved to make things easier for the family.

Often, Shane and dad would get together and party. Shane would often take me and his son's money, as usual, and use it for party expenses. I was numb to it at that point after happening for months on end. Shane, my dad, and their friend, Doug, liked to indulge in the limelight. They did this off and on for a while. One day, Doug saw me walking in the yard and pulled me aside, "Hey, I wanted to let you know that I have an apartment that you and your dad can stay in." I could not believe it! This was the best news I had ever heard because I would now have a room all to myself and a space where I could get everything I needed. I missed having a place to myself. Doug provided dad with everything he needed to take care of me. I was overjoyed. Doug was sick and tired of seeing me go through what I had experienced, and it meant so much to me to have someone have my back.

When we moved into Doug's duplex, it immediately felt like home. Finally, things were starting to look up. Then, hell broke loose. Apparently, Danielle got wind of what was happening and moved in with us. Great. When will I ever get a break? Obviously, I could not say anything without dad yelling at me, or Danielle making fun of me, so I stayed silent. So, dad let her in to stay with us. But the thing is, Danielle already had the resources she needed. Her mother and grandmother had places set up for her, but since she knew that I started to have things going for me, she did not want to feel left out. Unfortunately, Danielle was not the only one trying to weave her way in. Reba was pushing for Yazmen to come and stay with us also. And the worst part was they did not even care why we were here and why this place was opened only for dad and me. Happiness was there for a little while, and then I was back to my everyday normal.

Chapter 17

I was back at square one. What I thought was the perfect place to live had turned into what I had been experiencing my entire life; people abusing people, taking advantage of positive situations, and many more. There was an older lady who lived next door and started to complain about the noises we were leaving due to the abundance of unwanted visitors. This was much more than what she bargained for. She complained about everything; no matter if we were quiet, she complained about us going in and out as if she expected us to stay inside all day. She begged Doug to move us somewhere else so she could have her peace and quiet back. It's best to know that since Doug owned multiple properties, he did not charge us rent. However, since the lady continued to complain over and over, it got to the point where Doug wanted to move us so everything would stop.

But no surprise, we ended up moving again. Dad let Danielle pick the room she wanted, which was not fair since I was there first. But come on, I should not have been surprised because I always received the crap end of the stick, and there was nothing I could do about it. I mean, the only room in the house she could pick was the one that gave her privacy, so I guess I tried to understand from her point of view. Since dad was still traveling to High Point to see Reba, that left Danielle and me having free reign in the house to do whatever we wanted, whenever we wanted.

One night, Danielle and I were enjoying ourselves and having a good time. However, she started noticing not everything was gold on the other side. She noticed the unpaid bills started to rack up again, and dad left us both to fend for ourselves again. I was used to this already. She decided to ignore it and went back to having a good time.

One night, as we enjoyed the peaceful evening of just us, out of nowhere, we heard footsteps storming up to the house. Suddenly, dad stormed through the door and headed straight toward me. I had no idea what was happening. Dad took his hand and knocked me straight across the face.

"What was that for?!" I lashed out, confused as to why he would hit me out of nowhere.

"What are you doing?!" Danielle cried out to him.

He yelled back, "You do not be up here talking about me!" Staring at me with eyes filled with rage. We all began looking at each other, confused, unable to figure out what he was talking about.

"What are you talking about? We are not talking about you!" Danielle tried to defend me, but dad did not have it. Releasing myself from his grasp, I walked off to my room with tears in my eyes, still unaware of what had just happened and why. But after calming down, I decided to let it go.

With no surprise, things got worse as the months went on. Not wanting to experience any more of it, Danielle moved back in with her grandmother, leaving me to fend for myself since dad was still going between High Point and Hickory. His trips grew longer and longer, leaving me helpless and alone. Apparently, dad received a $1,200 check from a guy to take a trip with him to Arizona to find gold. When he went to Reba's and came back, he told me he booked a trip to Arizona to look for gold. Even with the utilities turned off, again, he cared more about spending his $1,200 on the Arizona trip than taking care of responsibilities at home. Once again, neglecting me. This time around, I was alone for a full week. What was I going to do? I did know one thing; whenever I needed something, I could walk there. Church, the grocery store, no matter where I needed to be, walking got me there all the time. Dad called me one morning to tell me the electricity bill was due and to go down to social services to have them assist with it.

With no food, lights, or heat, I was left alone, once again, with nowhere else to go. But thankfully, I had been in this situation before, many times over, and I knew what to do. I still spoke with Shane's son and hung out with him from time to time. Shane and his wife heard that I was staying at my house without the utilities on, and they offered to let me come and stay with them again. Knowing the only food, I had in the house was lunch meat, I accepted their offer. Staying with them made my commute to my job at Food Maze easier. However, the same rules applied. On the other hand, though, I had a place to lay my head that had working lights, heat, and conditioning. This time around, Shane's family moved into a 2-bedroom house, so the only place I could stay was on a small space on the floor. Honestly, it was better than nothing. I had a place that opened its arms for me, and that meant more than anything.

Chapter 18

What I learned is that you never know what is going to happen. While I was at work one afternoon, I received a phone call that was out of the ordinary. Somehow, someone who had seen me working told my mother I was working at Food Lion, gave her the number to the store, and she called. We had not spoken in a long time, and I was shocked to even hear from her. What did she want? After talking for a little bit, she told me she wanted to come and take me shopping. I felt uncertain after the call because she called me out of the blue and wanted to see me. However, I went along with it to see what would happen. The next weekend, she pulled up in a red jeep and was ready to take me shopping.

"Are you ready? I will take you wherever you want!" I was down for that because who would ever say no to a free wardrobe? But what she said next took me by complete surprise.

After she picked me up and we went on about our business she about a few hours of relaxing she asked me was a gay. I was absolutely taken aback. I looked at her as if she had lost her damn mind. I could not even put the right words together – my mind went blank, and my mouth stood still. I tried to put a proper response together, but all that my body could immediately say was, "No! What made you think that?"

"Don't you dare lie to me. I will ask again, and if you say yes, I will shove you out onto the highway without caring if anyone sees!" What could I possibly have done to protect myself at that moment? She had control of the vehicle, speeding down a crowded highway, and I was being interrogated by my mother. But I stuck to my guns and told nothing but the God honest truth.

"No, I am not gay!" She believed me after that, or at least I hoped. That was the weirdest, most uncomfortable conversation I have ever had with someone. Even after that, I still went with her to go shopping, and she bought me new shoes, clothes, and even a new cellphone. Even after the near-death experience I had earlier with almost being thrown out onto a crowded highway, hanging out with her meant so much to me; I was grateful for what she provided to me, even after all the time that passed. When on the way back, she promised to take me back to Shane's. The icing on the cake was that with my new phone, she promised to continue to pay for my cellphone bill, and I would never have to worry about it. That was the cherry on top of a great but weird day.

A few weeks later, my phone was turned off due to not being able to pay the monthly bill. Yet again, another empty promise from my mother. I am also grateful to God for the materials he put in me. These materials are what make a great person and I am beyond blessed that they are naturally instilled in me. I want peace always and the Bible says in Matthew 5:9 that the peacemakers are blessed for they shall be called sons of God. Here am I, attracting even more blessings into my life. Here was my mother who abandoned me from such a young age and who is worthy of every blame for how much difficulty I faced in my life, but when she called to see me, I did so without hesitation. She did not keep her promise to take care of the phone bill but even when she calls after this, I would meet her with open arms. This is the spirit of greatness.

However, I was grateful for the job I had at Food Maze because my steady paycheck allowed me to keep up with the monthly expenses. But do not get me wrong, it was hard at times.

You see, shortly after taking a new job at a Hotel, Shane started to demand I give my checks to him. There were nights that ended unexpectedly because Shane came and demanded that if I did not give him my hard-earned checks, he would put me out on the street. What was I going to do? I made money, yes, but not enough to support myself in my own place. I had no other choice but to surrender my paychecks to Shane so he could waste them on partying. This happened for several months, and it took me to a breaking point. I wished I could have let such a toxic person in my life go and finally experience freedom from pain.

Chapter 19

When in life, there will be someone that a child can talk to and confide in. They are like a guardian angel, ready to listen always, ready to advise, and ready to help out when the need arises. For me, that was Tara. She was one of the faculty members at my high school. Often, she would check in on me and make sure everything was okay. She was also a member of Bright Star Church, so we already had familiarity with what was happening in my life. She was like a mother to me. A lot of the time, she worked behind the scenes to make sure I had everything I needed. As we spoke together, she learned that I had been sleeping on the floor, and after recently turning 18, I was one year away from getting my own apartment.

Time could not move any faster. After telling her this, she took the information straight to the school board. She argued that with the living situation I was in, I deserved to have the best environment possible to thrive in. Miraculously, the school granted me my own place to live. When I first found out, I did not tell a soul. I felt so blessed that all of the teachers worked behind the scenes to give me a furnished apartment, a place that was mine. A place that I could call home. A place I could enjoy without the stresses of family. Best of all, they paid my apartment's rent for several months upfront. I was overjoyed, and I knew Yvonne was looking at me from above, cheering me on. Yet again, God shows up in the middle of a tough time and reminds me 'son, I am with you in this.'

I was willing to do whatever it took to provide for myself. To make ends meet, I secured a second job working at the local arts and craft store, which helped me save more money and stay self-sufficient. While working at Food Maze and the local arts and crafts store, I also worked sometimes for the local food shop, also while going to high school full-time. But when the workload piled up, I knew taking on a third job was too much to handle. So, I made the decision to drop it and focus on Food Maze and the arts and crafts store.

After living in my new place for a little while, I wondered if or when I would let everyone know. To be honest, I was scared to do this because the last thing I wanted, or needed, was for them to be mad at me. Though I was grateful for what everyone did for me, I also did not want to upset who I had lived with previously. I was set to graduate high school this spring. So, this was a very critical time for me to focus on what's most important. I did not mention my apartment for weeks until the day I broke down and spilled the beans.

After working hard in school for the past four years, I went through many ups and downs. The most significant part was that I was still able to interact with both my school and church communities and successfully pursue school. But after the semester came to an end, senior prom, senior photos, and purchasing my cap and gown were just around the corner. But when looking at it all, one thing was missing: my family did not help with any part of the process. While at a family cookout, I told them of my upcoming graduation, and I found out mom was going to come and bring her new boyfriend, Dre. Unfortunately, everyone else remained standoffish about my big day, but I tried not to let it get to me. I was in a much better place. Thankfully, my Uncle Matt stepped in and said, "If you are graduating, then we all need to be there." When my cousin graduated the year before, everyone planned a cookout, and it was really fun.

Finally, the big day arrived. My mom was on her way with Dre, and since I had never seen him before, I did not know what to expect or how to feel. A few months ago, my mom also shared with me that Sidney was not my real dad; Dre was. I was beyond confused and was not sure what to do in this situation. Even though my dad and I have been through many hurdles together, I was grateful for the small things. With that, I ignored the statement that Tyrone was not my real father. I chose to focus on my big day instead. As the class of 2005 stood in line, I saw mom and Dre enter from the side. I hardly recognized her since I had not seen her for years. Only three people showed up from my dad's side: Janet, dad, and my great aunt Cara from Shelby. She was Yvonne's youngest sister. I would have given anything to have Yvonne there for my graduation. She would've been so proud of me and what I accomplished.

After the ceremony, I was pulled between both families for congratulations and hugs, I did my best to balance it out and spread the love, so no one feels left out or isolated. Leyka stepped forward, "Hey! Let's go out to eat with me and Dre." Being that Leyka was never there during the years, I chose to go with my dad and his family, and we went to a local buffet. I thought it was very thoughtful of them to take me out to celebrate my graduation; it meant so much to me. But once I got there, with no surprise, I was expected to pay for not only my meal but my dads also. This was when Golden Ridge's all-you-can-eat-buffet was only $9.99. I did not get it. Out of all the times I was there to give him my paychecks from working, he had to do this during the one day when it was about me. I felt like I was the acting parent. I just swallowed the horse-sized pill and tried to enjoy the rest of the night.

Chapter 20

A few months had passed after graduation, and I was working more than ever before. But with working in a full-time capacity came with its fair share of challenges. I received two college acceptance letters, and I was so excited about this new adventure. However, college comes with paying for it, and finding funding was going to be a huge hurdle to overcome.

Being that I was still underage, I was unable to apply for loans on my own. I asked my dad if he could be a co-signer, and he said that he would do it, but it was nearly impossible to get in touch with him. It got to the point where he finally told me that I could not use his information in my financial aid applications. This screwed up my entire process. When I spoke with my mother, I asked her if I could use her information. She was hesitant and told me that I could not use her information.

After returning to school, I realized that I had to take matters into my own hands. So, I continue to do what I could to take care of myself. I wish I had held back from expressing how I felt because my school reached out and informed me that I still needed my parent's information to confirm my enrollment. I had no choice but to return to my mother and tell her what the school said. "Ask your dad" was her response, followed with, "I can't give you what they are asking for."

Before I turned away to leave, she left her final remark that really hit the nail in the coffin. "You are too dumb to go to college. Join the service, and they'll pay for your education. Then you can send me money and take care of me."

The devil does try to be a pain in the life of a person and when he shows his face to you, it is best for you to quickly identify him just as he is. The identity of a man is one very important aspect of his life that should never be toyed with. Listen, your identity is that mirror with which you look at yourself. It defines the steps you take, the decisions you make, and the moves you take. A person who identifies as a thief would not spend his days and nights in the chapel, praying. Likewise, a person who identifies as a holy priest would not spend his days and nights breaking into the houses of people and stealing their belongings. Your identity is very important to you, to God, and also to the devil. The devil knows that if he can alter your identity in a way that pleases him, then he can get you to walk out of the plan that God has for you. He says so many things to you, so many lies, and tries to destroy the identity of God in you. He says you are a loser, you are a poor man, you are unintelligent, you can never get a first-class degree, you are too dumb to go to college, you are a waste, you are not worth it, you do not deserve it, and so much more. Yes, all of these, when repeated over time and allowed to sit in your subconscious, they begin to form a solid stance in your mind. They begin to erase what God has told you and sound like the truth to you. The Bible says in 1 Peter 2: 9-*10 'But you are a chosen generation, a royal priesthood, a holy nation, His own special people, that you may proclaim the praises of Him who called you out of darkness into His marvelous light; who once were not a people but are now the people of God, who had not obtained mercy but now have obtained mercy.'* I want you to know that no matter what the world says to you or about you, you have an identity in Jesus Christ. The world will call you names, look down on you, and do all it can to keep you down, but remember this, you are not who the world says that you are, you are who God says you are. You are loved, you are special, you are protected, you are wise, you are great, you are not weak, and you are strong. This is what God says. Learn to shut your ears to everything the world has to say and open your heart to the saying of the Lord. Your life is in the hands of God, not in the hands of man. Nothing a man does or says will change the trajectory or direction of your life towards greatness, except if you allow it. If you are deeply rooted in your truth, you will not be easily moved.

It was at that moment that I realized my mother never truly cared about me, my education, or my well-being. She only cared about herself. It did not matter if I earned a valuable education or worked full-time somewhere. As long as she was taken care of, that's all that mattered.

After a while had passed, I did everything I could to show my parents that I did not need their support to make things happen for myself. When I graduated high school, I landed an exciting gig as a pastry chef at a local hotel. My grandmother was a baker for many years, and her delicious cakes always brought back wonderful memories. When I got this pastry chef job, I knew I wanted to follow in her footsteps. During my last first few weeks at the hotel as an intern, the Executive Chef took me under his wing, and I was able to learn so much. It was one of the most exciting and rewarding jobs I have ever had. I stayed with the hotel for a few years after that.

Chapter 21

It was just a few weeks before my 21st birthday, and I was asked to run for council. This was a big thing for the city as I was the youngest to ever run. Many people were standing behind me, and a few days later, they received the news I was just a few days short of being at the age limit to run. Again, another door opens unto me, clearly the work of God.

Over the next few months, there were oftentimes I spent time with my brother in the evenings, which I cherished and loved to do. I was also working a third shift job that was just a few minutes around the corner from where dad lived. Being that I had worked as the pastry chef at the local hotel, I was also offered the opportunity to work at one of the local craft stores as a floral designer.

I would oftentimes have people ask me to make a cake or flower arrangement for their special event. One of Bright Star's members asked me to help do their wedding. Since I had already assisted with a few weddings before, this was something I found exciting. It was time for the wedding, and everything looked amazing. They got through the wedding, and there was an issue with payment. Unfortunately, I had never been in a position before where I never received payment for completing a service. Because of the heart and soul that I put into the work I did, I pushed forward and refused to allow it to keep me from providing the services. Everything turned out and looked great in the end.

Over the past few years, many opportunities presented themselves to me. The church secretary helped me connect with many contacts. I worked with silk flowers over the past few years but never actually worked with real flowers before. One of the local florists that provided business to the church offered to let me come in and work with her for a few days to learn something about making real flower arrangements. This was an exciting opportunity that I did not want to pass up.

Over the next few days, I learned a lot from her. She offered to pay me, but I spotted a vase in the shop that I really liked instead. It looked just like one of the vases she recently made for the church. It also matched the colors that the school had provided me for the apartment. When I asked the lady for the vase, she did not hesitate, instantly saying yes. When she got the opportunity to use the vase for a special event, she ordered three and picked Bright Star to use two of the vases there and had one left over; so, when I asked to have it, she let me. I was incredibly grateful she let me keep it.

Several months passed, and I received a phone call from the church secretary. Apparently, I learned the church custodian had broken one of the vases, and she called the florist, and they let her know that she had given the last one to me. She asked me if I would be willing to sell it to the church. She did not sound happy while on the call. She explained to me that she reached out to the lady that ordered to vase, and she made a comment that I had stolen the vase from the church. I would have never been able to afford the vase. She explained to the lady that the situation was nowhere near what happened and that I would not need to steal anything from the church.

Hearing this shocked her. I had never taken anything from anyone and would not dare steal anything from a church. Although this hurt me greatly, I did not let it stop me. Being that I had also been promoted to the floral department at the local craft store, I was also making flower arrangements for the church as well. The lady that accused me of stealing the vase from the church also called a few other members to spread false information. The lady who was currently doing the flowers asked to come to my apartment. I invited her in, and she saw arrangements that I had been working on for the church. She instantly told him I needed to take all the stuff back up to the church. Because I did not want any issue, and since I did not understand what was going on, I grabbed the items and took them to the church. The church secretary asked me what was going on, and I explained to her that the rumors that were spread about me were about me taking stuff from the church, which she already knew was not true. This is very important in saying that when walking towards the plan God has for you, you must **always** have your hands clean. The devil wants to steal away your future and steal away the glory that God is reserving for you. He wants to creep in on you and catch you unawares but when you have your hands clean, you will be vindicated. You must learn 'consistency' because it is the key to true and unshaken greatness. You should not be bad and good; pick a side and stick to it! The Bible says in Revelations 3: 15-16, *'I know your works, that you are neither cold nor hot. I could wish you were cold or hot. So then, because you are lukewarm, and neither cold nor hot, I will vomit you out of My mouth.'* God needs to know what side you pick, and he can't tell when you keep going back to the bad side and doing a few bits of good here and there. Truly, good habits are not formed in a day; they take resilience and dedication to be formed but would you rather be sent away from the presence and watch of God when you are found wanting, hands deep in wrongs? No! Live carefully and free yourself from the hold of the wicked one.

The church secretary called the lady who went to my apartment and explained the situation to her about the vase and what had happened. She also explained to her that because I took my time, she allowed me to take the stuff home and work on it, and when I was finished, I would bring it back to the church.

The lady then understood what was happening and what was going on. Over the next few months, she began to work with me, and we became a great team, putting arrangements together until she decided to step down from the position and allowed me to take over. This was a great opportunity for me as I now had the chance to shift gears a little bit. No matter what it was, I always shared my gift with the church. This was my way of giving back to them.

Chapter 22

Christmas season was upon us, and I made a new friendship with one of my classmates named Renee. She was down to earth, and I enjoyed spending time with her. We hung out at her apartment a lot, which was a time I cherished with a great friend. Since she was disabled, I always helped her whenever I could. Especially since she recently had a newborn son, I told her to never be afraid to ask me to help. What was so special for me was that she asked me to be her son's Godfather. Without hesitation, I happily accepted and was excited to take on this new responsibility. Every Sunday, I picked up her son and took him to church with me, which was something we loved doing together. Even though he's only my godchild, I was always willing to do anything for him. He was, and is, my pride and joy. My life was making more sense, and even if the saying goes 'you can never give what you do not have', God filled my heart with so much love, that I was able to spread it to the people all around me.

It's Christmas Day, and dad's family decided to gather at my apartment. The last time we were all together, we met at Janet's house, and she and her daughter were rude to people. Since Yvonne's death, the family had not held a family dinner that was same as before because not everyone was invited to the ones we had; it just never felt right to have it without her. Although my apartment was on the smaller side, everyone sat around and seemed to have a good time. This was what family should have always been about from the beginning. Also, the family was excited for February since I was expecting a new baby brother. Dad was expecting his fourth child, which would mean the family had more than 30 grandchildren. What a blessing!

After the holidays, it was Super Bowl Sunday, and guess who decided to make his grand entrance? My new brother, Jayden. Of course, when a new baby enters the family and greets the world with his presence, everyone can't help but share in the excitement. Thankfully, mom and baby were doing well, which was important! Even dad ex-wife, Chanda, put her differences aside and helped to make sure Jayden had a safe beginning. When he got home safely, he stayed by his mom's side and received everything he needed. Do you know what was special about that? Not only did a beautiful baby boy enter the world with no complications, but everyone put their differences aside to create a welcoming environment for a new family addition. Over the next few months, exciting things remained consistent for me, especially when I spent time visiting my brother in the evenings. I worked a third-shift job that was just a few minutes around the corner from where my dad lived so this was easy for me.

Chapter 23

As the months went on, I never let anything stop me; I took to finding any chance I could to find the peace that I had always pushed forward. I continued to work the third shift job, which helped me save enough money to buy a car. Now I felt like I had the freedom to go wherever I wanted without having to rely on anyone else. Thankfully, dad worked on cars, so I could always go to him for repairs if I ever needed anything; however, as usual, he never had "time" to help.

Several months passed; still on the move. I began staying at my dad's house with my brother, but when I thought things were going well, shortly after I got my car, the contract for my third-shift job ended. That left me without any income to live off; I was desperate to make ends meet. On the other hand, though, what seemed like endless struggles in my life shined a light at the end of a long, dark tunnel. My brother and I were able to bond differently than we had before. Jayden was my pride and my joy.

Oftentimes, when we were alone, I listened to church music with Jayden. He was too young to understand what was happening around him, but when I drummed my feet to the music, Jayden copied me, praising God around the house.

Funds were tight to take care of Jayden after seeing dad run away to the basement and party every weekend. His weekends of partying made him spend hundreds of dollars without realizing the house was already burning money. I was not sure what to do and I was willing to do whatever it took to get money, so I began to look into options to sell the party supplies that my dad was buying. Since he was giving it to someone else why not make myself available and at my dad's friends convenience? This took place over several months. I was making good money bringing over $3,000 in just 4 days. I could get use to this, all I had to do was just stay in one place and not move at all. My dad was my biggest supporter.

Over the next few months things began to get better. Money was coming in pretty fast. I was able to pay my car down and pay up a few extra bills. But one night, as I was driving home and not paying attention to the road, I wrecked my car and totaled it. This was a major eye opener for me. Over the next few months, I realized that the fast money that I was making had begun to go just as fast as I was getting it and one of the results was the car he had lost. This life wasn't for me either. I learned that when I made my money the right way, I would be able to save and keep the things I had received and made for longer. I learned that I was able to appreciate thing he got as well.

Chapter 24

The Word of God says in Deuteronomy 28: 12-13, '*The LORD will open to you His good treasure, the heavens, to give the rain to your land in its season, and to bless all the work of your hand. You shall lend to many nations, but you shall not borrow. And the LORD will make you the head and not the tail; you shall be above only, and not be beneath, if you heed the commandments of the LORD your God, which I command you today, and are careful to observe them.*' Yes, God knows His own and He will move mountains to take care of each of his children. But what He will not do is condone or allow for laziness! Even God, the king of the world, is not lazy. He worked for six days to get the heavens and earth ready for habitation, and if any man thinks that they will be pampered and spoon-fed because they are children of God, then they have it wrong. Genesis 1: 26-28 says '*Then God said, "Let Us make man in Our image, according to Our likeness; let them have dominion over the fish of the sea, over the birds of the air, and over the cattle, over all the earth and over every creeping thing that creeps on the earth." So, God created man in His own image; in the image of God, He created him; male and female*

He created them. Then God blessed them, and God said to them, "Be fruitful and multiply; fill the earth and subdue it; have dominion over the fish of the sea, over the birds of the air, and over every living thing that moves on the earth.' What does that tell you? The same likeness of God that was used in creating the world, you and I were created in it. You have been given the power to change your life and to make it whatever it is you want it to be. You have the grace to create and multiply, and to make a great life for yourself. If God has invested so much in you, why would he still go ahead to spoon-feed you? He wants you to think, to work, to make moves that will move you from where you are to where you want to be, and then, He will bless the works of your hands and cause your work to prosper.

I never let anything stop me from striving to do what I needed to do to make it. A local call center came to town, an exciting big move for our city. I did not have much experience in a call center, but I put my best faith-filled foot forward and applied for one of the positions. Within a few days and with a lot of faith, I was offered the job. I loved the team I worked with because everyone treated each other like family, and we established an amazing bond. This was something I had never experienced before. The group always got together and had fun; we supported each other, and over time, our bond became stronger.

Later, I started feeling severe stomach pains, and I became worried about what was going on. I had never experienced something like this before. The pain lasted for several weeks. I asked members of my church to pray for a fast and easy recovery, but two of the members said that the reason for my stomach pains was due to having AIDS, which was obviously incorrect. However, they spread this information like wildfire. I was incredibly hurt by their immature behavior, but I pushed forward. Surprisingly, this was not the worst thing to happen to me. After a while, the rumors stopped, and the two members who started the rumor turned their hatred onto me, being rude every chance they got.

As a child, I always leaned on the church to be my safe space and the only place where I could find comfort. Unfortunately, now, it was pushing me away. One thing about me was I never minded praising God—his praise got me through a lot. But when I praised God, some members of the church told me it did not take all that and that I needed to sit down somewhere. But the more they tried to sit me down, the harder I praised God's name. You see, they did not understand the battle I was dealing with inside. Many people did not know the suicide battles I had to conquer, and the only thing that held me together was where I could make it to church and be in the presence of God. Many did not understand the battles I went through. Many times, I remained quiet about things that I went through. Being that my mother rejected me, and I became the black sheep of my dad's side of the family, everything was hard. All I wanted was to be loved.

Recently, I went over to Shane's house to hang out. All of his friends, brother, and son were visiting from Virginia and were sitting around. Shane's daughter, Ashley, and her cousin came in from out of town and made comments about my skin color, how dark I was. I have always been sensitive about my skin, especially after how my mother rejected me due to it.

There was nothing I could do about the color of my skin, and I tried to not let the comments bother me. Because my mother rejected me in the past when I dealt with the issues of the color of my skin, on top of the school bullying I endured, the more I tried to block it out, the faster the jokes and comments came. "Look how black he is," they'd say, or "You can't even see him in the dark," or, "He looks like a tar baby," and one added, "Call him blacky." When you thought school was the one place that picked on me and bullied me was just scratching the surface. After a while, the tag-teaming heavily weighed on me, and then the negative racial remarks did not help. Then when they commented about how I would go home and cry, I did not let their words affect me.

Why me, though? No matter where I went or what I did, I was always the target of bullying. My dad's side of the family held a family dinner in Shelby, North Carolina, and I did not go. It was like walking on eggshells around them, and because I chose to not go, a few of the family members decided to make me the topic of conversation. If I went, they would make side comments and talk about me, and if I still was unable to go because of work, they would still sit around and talk about me. Someone in the group called me and put me on speaker phone, so I could hear what was said. In the background, a woman said she was going to leave if they continued to speak about me the way they were. I could not believe what they were saying – their own flesh and blood. Everything that Yvonne told me finally came to light. I felt like an outsider and knew there was nothing I could do about it because all I was doing was being myself. My own family could not show me that they loved and cared for me, and it really showed when I was not there. I was the black sheep.

I worked hard to get to where I was in my life, and with God on my side, I pushed for greatness. At that point in my life, many people told me I would never be anything, never make it out of high school, never make it in life, never become anything. But I always pushed for what was needed to take care of myself. Although it was never easy, I pushed harder each day.

My dad never did anything for me without payment from me. I decided to take care of myself by getting a new SUV, so I did not have to depend on him anymore. I had asked him to go with me to look at a car for several days in a row, and he always presented any and every excuse not to go. It's sad that a father desperately did everything he could to avoid being with his son; whatever, I moved on. When I asked him the last time to come with me, Karen sat there and heard my dad provide every excuse in the book why he could not go. Karen got up and went off on him in response, "This is not fair to him! He has been asking you to go look at this SUV for a while, and all you do is blow him off. If he was one of those girls you would break your neck to go see, you'd never do it otherwise. The least you can do is go and look at the SUV." By the time she was done fussing at my dad, he reluctantly agreed. But by the time he decided to go, the location was closed for business. It sucked because every chance I had the opportunity to do anything with him, I had no choice but to remain positive and move forward with the alternative option. I decided to get the truck. Every chance my dad had to drive the truck; he would do what he needed. I stopped letting him take the truck. I always had to pay other people to work on my truck and being that my dad would help fix or do anything to the truck, I stopped letting him drive it.

I told him, "You are comfortable with running my SUV down and not helping me fix it, so you do not get to drive my truck." Let's just say this was the last time I ever asked my dad to do anything for me. Looking back, the last time my dad did anything for me was years ago. He never provided anything for me, but I never asked him for anything because I knew it would never happen.

You can notice the pattern of me becoming a man for myself, gathering my experience over the years. I did not have to have a hard heart towards anybody, no. All I needed to do was take a strong stance and decide what was best for me, best for my growth, and best for my future.

Chapter 25

Several months passed, and I stayed at that apartment for years. I built great relationships with the maintenance team and established strong bonds with neighbors. For years, I noticed that they would randomly pop up at my apartment without notice, and there was nothing I could do about it. I eventually came to find out that the lady sent them over to my apartment when I was not there. She began to target me, and even the maintenance crew let me know what was happening. I never had traffic, drugs, or anything of the sort coming inside or outside my apartment. I always paid my bills on time. I did not understand why she was doing what she did to target me. I worked on several projects at home and had her show up in the middle of them. It got to the point where I did not want to stay in my own apartment anymore, but I had no choice but to deal with her. Later, it came to light that one of the staff members knew of my savings, and apparently, it was the largest one their tenants ever had. If they found a way to get me out of the apartment, I would have lost it all. I had to find a way out there for good.

In the midst of all this, plus getting sick again, I received a job offer to work at one of the largest banks in Charlotte, North Carolina. This big change from what I had before could now open up so many doors. Immediately, without hesitation, I jumped on the opportunity. My new job was everything I had hoped and prayed for. Although the new job kept me busy traveling back and forth, I remained active in the church. I had the best of both worlds. But then, the honeymoon phase after accepting a new job began to fade, and the real struggles that come with marriage took the stage. The long rides to and from work began to take a toll on me. Even though I enjoyed the job, I began to look for places between Hickory and Charlotte so my commute time would be shorter. Plus, the continuous harassment from the lady at the office had me ready to leave the apartment. Unfortunately, time was not my friend in this case.

After several months of stress and getting everything out of the apartment, I finally reached the finish line; I moved out. When everything was out of there, the lack of attention and maintenance this apartment had was appalling. Personal items were left, covered in mold. The property refused to replace or pay for any of the items that were damaged and only remained upset because of the $6800.00 check they had to award me. They found a loophole that kept them from replacing the damaged items. Because I never gave up, I attempted to take the apartment complex to court, but it fell through, and let me tell you, I enjoyed living in my new place. Everything was going well; nothing was damaged, and life seemed like it was going great. Then I got a phone call from a friend that the apartment complex stole some money and got into a heap of trouble. When you try to take from someone and do someone wrong, it comes back on you ten-fold. Because the apartment was caught embezzling money, they had to upfront hundreds of thousands of dollars rather than doing what was right.

I realized then if I stood still and let God fight my battles, he would do more than you ever thought possible. *This is God*, I said to myself. You have to be careful about how you treat people because when they try and do you wrong, stand still and let God handle the situation. Do not let people change you. Do not let your experiences change who you are and what you stand for. When Jesus was down here on earth, He was bruised, stepped on, and insulted but He never turned His heart against people; in fact, He prayed for them that their sins be forgiven. Look, no man can reward you with a gift as permanent and significant as the gift that God will reward you with. The plans He has for you are so huge and so great, so you must never allow any man to push you to a point where you lose it all. Build your heart in God and around the things of God, build a character that will stand the test of time and frustrations from the people around you, then watch how God will continually lift you up far beyond your wildest expectations.

Chapter 26

I eventually gave up on the former apartment complex in trying to get my stuff replaced, and I started thinking about how I was going to replace the items in my home with the money I was awarded. My Aunt Janet reached out to me, and we talked. It was nice. I told her about what was happening with the apartment, and she agreed that I did the right thing to get out there when I did. She also heard about the money I received from them, and she hinted she found a used all-white sofa set she really wanted for her home and that she did not have the money for it. She asked me to loan her $1,000 to get the sofa set, and she would pay me back in installments. I told her that the money was already allocated for the things I needed, but I addressed if I had anything left over, I would let her use it. She became very persistent and insistent about getting the white sofa set before getting the things I needed. I had priorities I had to address first. I focused on getting everything I needed for my apartment, and Aunt Janet did not hesitate to express her frustration because I did not move as fast as she wanted me to. Because I was not moving as fasted as she wanted me to, she took it as her opportunity to not affiliate herself with me. This was all because I focused on what I needed first before I let her use the money for herself. I did not realize how I transitioned into my place affected other people so much.

After several months passed, I stopped in to visit my brother. I went by the school and was informed that he was not doing well, that he was sleeping in class and coming to school dirty, and that his teachers were concerned. Over the next few weeks, I drove up from Charlotte to Hickory each day to sit with my brother to see what we could do to help him turn things around and do better in school. I went to the school daily for more than two weeks to check on him, and it came to where I could not make the drive anymore. We had a conference with one of Jayden's teachers, and while we were there, who worked as a teacher, we had a private conversation after the conference with the teacher where we learned about stuff that was going on in the household. Karen revealed all of this stuff to me.

Things have gotten so much worse for dad as his drinking became out of control, and it began to take a toll on our family. As we addressed the family friend, Karen let her know that the drinking was out of control and that if she could get him to take a pill, it could help him stop drinking. She also explained that he had a pot that he threw up in every morning and night when he drank. By this time, we were both in tears because I did not know all the things, she was sharing had opened up about. Dad was really bringing down the family a lot. She told us both that she did not want him knowing anything about the fact she was sharing this information with us and that he would do something to her if he ever found out. The family friend offered us support and help if she were to leave him. She stepped in to promise her to make sure she was good, but Karen decided to keep everything as it was and focus on trying to get him to take the pill. Unfortunately, dad never liked taking pills, but it was her decision.

Not sure what to do, I asked my dad if he could take my brother and let him stay with me so he could get what he needed. It was only during the week, dropping him off on Fridays and taking him with me on Mondays to make sure he needed everything when school was in session and was able to focus. During the weekend, holidays and summer, he could be with them. I offered to take him during school. But of course, dad's pride would not let me help. He felt that I was trying to take his son away from him, but this was not the case. This made dad feel some type of way. I did not know what else to do but reach out to two of dad's close friends and ask them to talk to him. When they met and talked with him, dad felt some type of way, saying he would think about it. I let him know that it was either me or the alcohol, and he chose the alcohol over me. Over the next few days, dad decided not to get help, and he spoke with his oldest daughter and sister, Janet who he had become very close. She was still mad at me for not paying for the white sofa. They teamed up against me and told dad he was a grown man, and he could do whatever he wanted, and if he did not want to seek help, which was his choice.

I had also been carrying the kids on my taxes. For two of the kids, I was only receiving $4,500, and I gave my dad $2,200 of it but Dad felt like I should give him more. Because of the white sofa deal, Janet had to jump in the middle of something that has nothing to do with her, even though she had the wrong information. I realized she would do anything she could to completely turn the family against me. And it worked. I did not get invited to any of the family events or anything that they had going on. If I ever did hear about a family event, it would only be after the fact.

Chapter 27

Several months had passed, and I continued to push forward. Over the past several years, I realized a lot. I began to see things that were happening to me and understood why these things happened. I learned only to move when I was told to move. This had been a not-so-easy process for me. One of the local pastor's daughters was getting married, and they asked me to do the wedding—I was so excited! A few years ago, I had the chance to do the parent's vow renewal service. One of the members of Bright Star Church, who was spreading rumors about me, was at it again. She did whatever she could to tear me down, and the saddest part was I had never done anything to her in my life, but it was almost like she could not bear to stand in my presence. At that moment, I realized that no matter what I did or how hard I tried, I could never make people happy no matter what.

Over the past few months, I have been working on the pastor's daughter's wedding. I drove over an hour several times a week to make sure they had what they needed. The family had so many obstacles that came up but kept moving forward. The location for the reception had closed its doors and was in search of a new place. The one they originally chose was smaller, so it would not require as many decorations. But now, being that they were going to have to find a new location, it was going to be more expensive since the location would be larger and would require more decorations.

As the family moved forward, funds began to tighten for them since the unexpected changes had taken a toll on their finances. I understood the situation and saw this as a moment where I could bless the family. Over the past few years, while at Bright Star Church, they had always been a blessing to me, so I made it my chance to give back. I told the family I would charge them $500 to do everything for the wedding, meaning everything they bought I got to keep, and they agreed. Out of the $500, there were four ladies who were paid $100 each and then a camera guy who was paid $125, although they only had to pay 500.00 the total for staff came to $525.

As time grew closer to the wedding, they laid out the design changes and found out large centerpieces were needed for the new location. Because they increased their guest list, it also called for more decorations. I still understood the situation and moved forward with getting the items that were needed to make the wedding a success. Sometimes as an event planner, you have to do what you can to still be able to deliver the quality of work that is needed for advertisement. There were several large arrangements, and I grabbed a lot of linen that I purchased to give the wedding some color. The linen alone cost over $1,400, and I asked them to pay $75 for the cost of the linen. Since the family told me they could pay the $75, they upfronted $50 of it, promising the remaining $25 later on, but it never came. The bride also had a conversation with me about how her mom was pushing her to get married because she and her boyfriend were living together, and it did not look good to the family. That put a lot of stress on her, and it felt like she was being pushed into something she did not want to do; however, she did not want to make her mother and stepfather angry. They both had seen each other in the local store and spent almost an hour talking about different obstacles that kept coming up. She repeated how she was being pushed into this wedding and felt like it was her mother's wedding the entire time. I explained to her that at the end of the day, this is a life decision that she had to make, and she will have to live with it. I told her to make the right decision and do what was best for her.

It was a month before the wedding, and I noticed that both the bride's and her mother's demeanors changed toward me. There was information I had asked about, and it was like it was being kept a secret. I began to not feel right about the entire thing, but it was too late for me to back out since I had already spent $4,500 out of my own pocket for the wedding. I wanted it to look good. The bride and her mother were set to visit my home to see some of the work I did, but I felt something was not right; I could not put my figure on it. Something told me not to let them visit. I prayed about it, and it weighed heavily to not let them visit, so I went with my gut feeling and reached out to them to let them know I was not going to be available. Obviously, they weren't happy. In fact, this only added more fuel to the fire that was already boiling. By this point, I felt good about my decision of not letting them come to my home, but now both the bride and her mother became extremely hateful toward me. By this time, I was ready to get the wedding over with. I had already spent so much money, and the family was nothing but hateful and rude to me, even after everything I had done for them.

Still confused about what was going on, I did not say anything at all. I asked the bride to pick up clear soda for the centerpieces since it would give the tall centerpieces an awesome bubbling effect, and she agreed to use her food stamps to get them. A few days later, she came to me and told me she was unable to get them. Still working toward making everything look nice, I moved forward with getting the rest of the items needed, including the drinks the bride could not get. I also asked for the times that the wedding cake and caterer would arrive, and thankfully, she provided both arrival times. She also decided to do a seating chart for the wedding but was delayed in providing it. She agreed to print the table numbers at the daycare her mother worked for, so I moved on and pushed toward the finish line for the big day.

Finally, it was time for the wedding rehearsal, and I had made it to the church on time. However, the rudeness escalated, and it really took a heavy weight on me. I never had a bride act like this before, a true bridezilla. With everything going on, she took her anger out on the one person who did everything they could to make the wedding happen.

I sat in the lady's lodge at Bright Start where the wedding was going to take place, lights off and in the dark. I prayed and asked God to get me through the wedding and to help me hold everything together. While sitting in the lodge, the bride walked in with her girls. She stared at me and looked in the mirror to check herself out as they prepared to walk out of the room. My grandmother always taught me that if you walk into a room and someone is in there, you speak with respect. But as the bride got ready to walk out of the doorway, she swung her head around, looked at me, and said, "Hey, Bernard" in the rudest tone and voice, as if she was the queen and I was her slave. I spoke in a calm voice, "Hey." and she left the room with her girls, cutting the light back off.

By that time, the bride and her mother continued to spread rumors about me, but the Holy Spirit calmed me, even in the middle of that mess. I learned that if you stand still and allow God to fight your battles, he will do more damage than you could ever imagine. If you tried to handle it yourself, you could only make a mess out of it. Finally, it was time for the rehearsal to start, which lasted around 45 minutes. Because I wanted to get this over with, I rushed through the rehearsal. Soon as it was over, I dashed out, no longer wanting to be a part of the drama. People wanted to put on a show to make others think they had it going on, which was not the case. I kept my mouth shut and moved on.

It was the morning of the wedding, and the bride and her mother got a hotel room to get ready. I was on my way to prepare for the wedding, but both the bride and mother called me to come to the hotel room. Already, they were up to no good. I could see right through what was happening, and I let them know that I was not going to have time to make it to them; Instead, I sent someone else, but they rejected the offer. They also asked if they could pay me with a check, and I refused. I knew that if I allowed them to pay with a check, they could stop the payments. That was what they had planned to do, being that they had financial issues already. I told them that they would have to have cash for me, and they had to pay for everything that I helped with since the check would not clear on time. Even though they both tried to push back, they agreed to pay with cash.

It was just a few hours before the wedding, and the venue put out black chair covers on the tables along with dirty tablecloths. I reached out to the bride to let her know what was going on, and she rudely told me that it was not her issue and that I needed to figure it out. There was no black at the wedding, so I had to ask them to change the table covers to white. As time went on that day, it was time for the cake and caterer to show up, but no one arrived. Apparently, the bride gave me the wrong time, so I asked one of the staff members to stay over until they arrived. There were also sticks that the bride purchased as tall centerpieces for the wedding. While they were being set up, one of the centerpieces was sitting under a light, and if the stick was used in the centerpiece, it would make it a fire hazard. So, my team decided not to put the sticks in the centerpieces and put them in the hallway. While they brought them over, the owner stopped them and asked if they would use the sticks since they sprayed glitter everywhere. Because of the mess, they would charge the bride a $350 fee to clean up the glitter since it was hard to get out. I told the team to put the sticks to the side, and they would deal with them later. I just wanted to move forward with everything.

Finally, it was time for the wedding to start, and one of the hosts walked up to me and told me the bride had instructed me to print the table numbers. Already trying to prepare for the wedding to start, I was confused because the last time they talked about table numbers, the bride was going to print them at her mother's daycare. But I decided there was not enough time to get it done, so I told my team not to worry about it and move on to the next item on the list. The wedding started, and things moved forward. Once the wedding was over, I got the wedding party prepared to take wedding pictures. I dashed over to the wedding reception area to make sure everything looked perfect. Months before the wedding, I offered to cut the wedding cake, which was something I had done at most weddings. This time, they let the cake caterer handle it, so I told my team not to do anything with the cake. As the reception was kicking over, I took some time to disappear and get myself together. When I stepped back in, I found out that the caterer ran out of food, and they had to go back and make more. Not only did they run out of food, but the guests were getting antsy when both food and drinks ran out. By that time, people came to me to complain, and there was nothing I could do about it; it had nothing to do with me. I started cleaning up the small things, so my team did not have much to do. I noticed that the sodas were left over. One of the ladies working with me suggested letting the wedding guests drink the sodas. I told them to let the caterer deal with it; I felt some type of way.

As rude and as nasty they had been to me, I shouldn't have to save face for them, but I did not want to stoop down to their level. By then, it became clear that the bride and her mother made it apparent to others how they were talking me down, but I continued to move forward. You could feel the tension in the air.

As they cleaned up, the bride began to grab things off the table. She stated, "I want this, and I want that" while rudely grabbing items. However, as agreed in the beginning, everything they bought I was supposed to keep. Ignoring everything that was agreed upon, the bride continued to grab things off the table, but she took a look at the cake, and somehow the cake topper and the top tier layer were mushed in the same box. Now, remember, I was never near the cake or had anything to do with it. The bride went to me, telling me how I messed it up, and I should have made sure it was put up correctly, and I reminded her that she never wanted me or my team to do anything with the cake. Even though I had nothing to do with the cake, the bride ignored me and continued to accuse me of ruining her cake. We both began to go at that time, but she continued to complain about everything, and in the midst of it, the groom's mother pulled me to the side and told me that I had a beautiful wedding; she enjoyed it and gave encouraging words. As we continued to clean up, the bride stuck around to continue to complain about her wedding. At that point, as she continued to complain, my team continued to clean and pack everything up. As we finished loading the last few things into the car, the bride stood outside the door with the groom and told me I did nothing right for her wedding and how I ruined everything. The groom grew tired of her complaining and told her that all she ever did was complain, and all she did was ruin his wedding night. She continued to go back and forth, but he eventually got her in the car, and they left. By this time, I was done with this wedding and no longer had anything to worry about or handle…

… or so I thought.

Chapter 28

A few days after the wedding, the bride's mother reached out to me, asking to talk. But since the bride treated me the way she did during the wedding, I was done talking to them, so there was no reason for us to talk anymore, knowing that none of this would ever be reconciled. I was over it, and it was already in the past.

Over the next few days, the bride was still angry about the wedding and was looking for small stuff to complain about. She even posted online that I had stolen her stuff from the wedding. The original agreement we had was that I was supposed to keep everything they bought. I had never stolen anything before in my life, so why would I need to do it now? She and her mother started spreading rumors again, and I did not react or make comments on the posts they made. She told me she was going to take me to small claims court over the sticks she was being charged for; even though the sticks cost $60, it was the fact that she kept this back-and-forth nonsense going. I offered to go to Judge Reid and called one of the reality TV show judges so we could take it on live television for all to see. I was going to countersue her for the $4,500 for the money I put into her wedding, willingly, since she was unable to afford anything. She declined that offer.

All I tried to do was help her, but she did not have it. Even though I was not paid a dime, even though they paid me $500, it all went to the staff I hired for the wedding. I knew that if I pushed back right then, it would put their business out and would make a mess of everything. So, I allowed God to fight this battle for me. Over the next several months, I received numerous phone calls about how the family was spreading rumors. Even one parent from the daycare whose child went there called me and allowed me to listen in on how the bride's mother was speaking about me. Everything she said was wrong, but I did not say anything. I allowed God to handle it. The lesson I learned was that the people you think would be the most grateful are actually the ones that make you feel like you owe them the world.

I continued to receive phone calls about the rumors they were still spreading about me, saying that I had stolen her stuff, pretty much performing great defamation of my character. In fact, the bride went over to one of my potential client's homes just to do what she could to take the business away from me. I did not allow the devil to take control of him, but I sat back and allowed God to give me a big bucket of popcorn and a front-row seat to see the show. A few weeks later, one day, while minding my business, I received a phone call. "Have you heard about the bride and groom?" I was asked. I said no, and I prayed all was well with them. Apparently, the rumors were still being spread about me, but I let God fight that battle. The conversation continued, and apparently, the couple split, and they were getting an annulment. The groom left her; their marriage did not even last three months. Then, I realized God was already fighting this battle. Over time, several things would occur and happen to this family. You can't go and treat people wrong and expect God to bless you. I simply prayed that God had mercy for them, but this battle was given to God, and it was no longer my problem to deal with. It was the Lord's.

Chapter 29

Later on, I continued to push forward as I received phone calls from people letting me know about what was going on. But there was nothing that could be done. It was very sad. Over the next few years, I had been driving back and forth to Bright Star, and I had not found a new church in Charlotte yet. One of my coworkers asked me to visit her church, but I continued to push her off. I had only been to Bright Star, and I had no plans of leaving just yet,

One Sunday, I did not feel like making the hour-long drive back home to Bright Star Church, so I decided to make the visit to her church. *Wow.* It was my only reaction because I had never been in a service where the spirit of God moved, and it was so high the spirit of God met you at the door as soon as you walked in. It was amazing. No one judged you for praising God; they joined in with you. This was a major difference from what I was used to. At Bright Star, they picked on me when I praised God, or they would tell me I was doing it too much and needed to sit down. Even though Bright Star was my home church, there was something about the new church that I could not stay away from. Each Sunday, I looked forward to just being in the midst of people that did not mind praising God. It was contagious.

Over time, I began to wean myself from going to my home church. For many years, that was the only church I knew. I lived and breathed that church. That was one of the many reasons I became the person I am today. I could have gone so many ways, but there were mothers that grounded me in the Lord that stepped out and did what they could to help raise me and make sure I had what I needed. The sad part was they really do not make church mothers like that anymore that did not mind getting dirty for the Lord.

As time passed, I began to visit and do more for the new church. There was nothing that could keep me from church, the place where I felt safe. I was keeping my focus on God; I did not mind working for the Lord. Many days and nights, I spent countless hours preparing the church for whatever was needed. I always made sure the house of worship was where it needed to be. Many times, I took time off from work to take care of God's house because when you do, he will take care of you. There was a time when I gave my last to the church, but because of God, somehow, I received more than I ever expected. Over the next few years, I continued to strive and work in excellence and do what was needed in the house of God. Even though many times I was taken advantage of, I did not allow that to stop me. Many challenges came and went, and I never let one stop me. I later found out that hard work would eventually pay off.

Chapter 30

After living in Hickory for several years, I moved to and lived in Gastonia, which was halfway between Charlotte and Hickory. Depending on the day, I did not have to drive as far. It reminded me of back home; since it was not too big, I was able to get to everything I needed in a timely manner.

After leaving here and cutting all ties with Hickory, I wanted to try the Charlotte thing. I have heard many people say that having a roommate could be a blessing or a curse. I had never really had a roommate, but I was willing to give it a try.

After doing some research and trying to figure out what area I wanted to live in, I found a roommate. I only wanted a 6-month contract just in case it was not going to work out. I would only have to deal with it for 6 months.

It started out good. The rules were to have no one extra in the home. No one was to use our restrooms. If we had someone else over, we respected each other and let us know before. Well, to make the story short, I started noticing that items in my bathroom were being used. Paper towels and tissues started going fast. At first, I thought it was me. Until one day, I came home early, and there was a group of people there walking in and out of my bathroom. It then hit me why I was buying a pack of paper towels and tissues each week.

I then removed all my personal things from the restroom as I felt violated at this point, but what can I say? This was his place, and there was nothing I could do. Two months before my six-month lease was up, the guy moved a girl he had met offline into the apartment with her children, and he had made it comfortable for them to use my restroom. The issue then became them playing with the water in the bathroom, missing the toilet, not cleaning the shower, and much more. I then realized that this roommate thing was not for me.

I told myself moving forward, if I could avoid it, I would not have another roommate unless it was someone that I was building something with. But I tried it. We should at least try things once before we knock them. It was an experience. There was something that happened that was good, and there was something that happened that was bad. I will be forever grateful for the experience. Unless it was a very temporary situation, I would not walk back down this road again.

Over time while looking for an apartment, I fell very ill. I was barely able to walk or breathe. As a result, I began missing work. It became very hard to push forward at times, and I wanted to give up. But I had to push forward for me. All I wanted to do was sleep because my body became so weak. I reached out to my doctor, and he was not sure what was going on either at the time. So, to make myself comfortable, I booked a hotel room and stayed there, so I did not have to deal with my roommate. My doctor asked me if I had been in a situation where I was constantly changing the temperature. I looked at him and realized that within the past 2 months, while my roommate was there, it would get really cold in the house. But then, when he left during summertime, he cut the air off, which made it get really hot in the house. The doctor diagnosed me with double walking pneumonia. He asked me how long I had been feeling that way, and I explained that it was around a month or more. Because of my answer, he told me to immediately go to the hospital since my oxygen levels were critically low. While I was in the hospital, my roommate reached out to me and asked if I would move out early so that they could get the kid's room ready for them. He was tired of them sleeping on his sofa. I told him I was not able to since I was in the hospital, but I would be out by the end of the month. In the midst of being in the hospital, I had to search for a new place to stay. On top of it all, my job messed up my check, and it would take a while for them to fix it so I could get paid.

Unfortunately, that resulted in me not getting paid for 3 pay periods, which let bills get behind. I had the option of not having a car or having a place to stay, but at that time, I did not have the energy to deal with it. Because of my work's error, I was not able to find a place to lay my head by the move-out date. For the first week, I was hurt and felt lost as to how I got in that position in the first place. But one thing we should always remember is that God sometimes puts us in situations where there is something he needs to show us, something very important he needs to teach us. The seed that is in a bag will never grow to bear fruits, and the gold that is never passed through a hot fiery furnace will never be valuable, likewise us! If we never pass-through situations and obstacles, we may never learn very important things that are necessary for our growth and progress in life. It is not always a bad thing, but more of a learning experience.

Chapter 31

I started living in my car, homeless. I asked God, "Why am I here in this place?" I remember I had been homeless twice before the age of 18. But this was the third time. I had money. I had a car. But why was I back here? It was like I wanted to apply for apartments, but there was something that would not let me. A few people offered me to stay with them while, at the same time, provided excuses. It did not matter because I would not move from this place until God was clear to me. If I did not know anything else, I knew he would not have ever put me in this place unless there was something he needed to show and for me to take from it. Oftentimes, we panic and try to work things out on our own. Sometimes when we try to fix it ourselves and make a mess of it, if we learn to trust God and his plan, it will all work out in our favor. I learned this firsthand. I am sure you know how things go before you get paid—you already have your check planned out. That check was going to be the check I used to move to my new place. But when I got paid because of the error, they messed up my check-up, so things did not go as I planned.

At first, I was upset and angry. So, I took matters into my own hands. I needed a shirt for work. So, I when to the local clothing store, and there was a guy outside. Let's just say we make mistakes that can be very costly. The guy had a small blackboard. If you guess what cap the chip was under, you get $300.00. This sounded so good, and every little bit helped. But you had to pay $100.00 to get into the game. At that point, I took my trust out of God and put it in this game. And what do you know? I lost. But I was not going to give up since I needed this money, and I needed to win back the money I lost. He told me if I gave him $500.00, then he would give me $1000.00.

I really needed that money. So, I went to the ATM and tried to get the funds out, but I was not able to; the ATM declined. I had the money in my account, but the machine would not allow me to get it. However, I was eventually able to get $300.00. So, I went to him, and I told him I could only get $300.00. I knew if I studied the caps, I could win. But what I did not know was that he had a trap under the board. Once again, I lost. By this time, he had walked about, and I noticed that the group of people that was standing around him had also walked away. I followed him, begging him to give me another chance, but I did not have any more money. The guy then pulled a gun on me. This had never happened before. I then took off running. He hopped in his car and sped off with the other cars following him. I was hurt and embarrassed. I realized at that moment that I had taken away my trust in God and put in the game. Had I kept my trust in God, I would not be in the situation that I was in. But because I made this costly gamble, it was going to be a major setback. Taking the wheel from God may seem logical a lot of times. You say to yourself 'oh, this ride is going too slow. There is my destination right there by the corner, so I should take control and just take one more turn right here'. That is the devil speaking to you. Listen, that turn will be a crash, I assure you. Again, remember that the plan of your life was made by God. You must learn to trust in Him always! When an engineer comes up with a design for some type of machinery, it is his idea. When he markets it out to people, no one in their right sense will say 'oh, I know how to make this thing work better than the owner, the engineer whose idea it is.' That would be plain silly. God knows best, never let Him out of your sight! Let's just say from this point forward, I just panicked and handled things on my own. However, I learned to seek God's face and stood still until his will was clear to me.

For several months, I took showers at my job and at the local gym and slept in my car. There was a local extended stay down the street, but they always stayed full. I went daily, but I was not able to get in. Because bills had gotten behind, I was not worried about an apartment. All I wanted to do was just get a place to lay my head. There was a lady that was working at the extended stay and asked me what was going on. I explained to her what had taken place. Sometimes, God strategically puts angels and people in place to work on your behalf. Before, when asking how I could get in, they kept telling me they had no openings and would not probably have any for a while. But I kept checking every day. After I talked to the lady and told her what was going on, she told me to come the next morning. She also asked me that if something came open would I have the money to pay for it, and I told her yes. The next morning, I was right there, and before I knew she was pulling me into a room. I realized that many times, during our hardest times, God will find a way to bless us more than we will even know. During this time, my eyes opened more than they had ever been. Without a place to lay my head, nobody even knew what was going on. Then the timing began to work itself out; I received a promotion on my job. I had only been on the floor for about 6 months. I knew it was not anyone else but God but doing his work.

A few months passed, and I went to a local big-time Gospel singer's local church. I did not have money to buy new clothes yet. During the time I spent sleeping in the car, I began to stress-eat, so a lot of my clothes became too small. By this time, the only thing that was pulling me through was church. If I could just make it to church, everything would be alright. One Sunday afternoon, I had on Carolina blue pants and a white blazer with a tie.

The pastor was known for giving away money to people. But I was not there for that. I needed to be fed the word of God. I noticed he kept looking at me. He was trying to get the minister of music to see. So, he offered to give me money, and in order to get it, I had to go to the front of the church. Before the money was offered, there was a lady that several people had sowed into her life. As I headed to the front of the church, I noticed he was just staring at me with a smirk on his face. I noticed he was waving at his minister of music to look at me, and when I got there, they both laughed. He gave me the money. After I received the money from him, I gave every single bit of it to the lady that everyone was sowing into. I needed it so much, but I also knew God will take care of me, so I gave all of her to her.

When I got back to my seat, he started talking down about people coming to his church dressed up in suits and things like that. He stated this was not that type of church. As a result, everyone began looking back at me, but I did not budge or move. I sat right there as if I did not know who he was talking about. When I left after service, I went home and cried. The one place - the church - that was supposed to be a safe place had once again let me down. The church should be the hospital, and it failed once again. This was not a reflection of God but a reflection of a man using God's house to make fun of and bully people. But I did not let it stop me. I stayed strong, and I prayed to God that there was a victory after this. The following Tuesday, I was at work, and I noticed the big boss was calling all of my team members into a room one by one. I had no idea what was going on. We are all looking at each other because we thought something was not right. Finally, my time came to walk the green mile. I went into the office, sat down, and she pulled out a paper before looking at me. My body began to shake because, Lord, this was the last thing I needed to lose my job. She started talking and began to say they had done some research and noticed that our pay was lower than the local market for the position I was in, and they were going to be giving me a $3.00 raise on top of my pay that I was already making. You can't tell me that we do not serve a God that sits high and looks low. I began to thank him right then and there. If He did it before, He could do it again. All we have to do is stand still in his word and know that He is God and trust Him.

By this time, I had begun to like the room I was in. I became very comfortable. I called it my studio with a maid. Once a week, they came into the room, cleaned it, and changed out the linen. I could get used to this. The area was right by my church and my job. It was the perfect place. Nobody bothered me, and I did not bother anyone else.

Chapter 32

A few months went by, and I was still not able to go back to the new church I joined under watch care. I found myself to be deeply focused on my church by making sure it had what it needed to run smoothly. There were a number of gifts that God provided to me, and if I used them right, they would build his kingdom. I took my time to build for the house of God and guess what I got in return, God was building my life! He was opening doors of blessings unto me, doors I did not even know existed. He was building me into a great and unshakeable lion, from the little kitten that I was while growing up. He was looking at my heart and giving it the right fixes that it needed.

There were countless times I wanted to walk away from the church. So many times, I wanted to walk away, but I had to remember that I was never there for the people. I was there for God; He was all I needed to stay sane and fulfilled in this cold world; my confidant and my hope. The key was to keep the focus on God, which was not always easy, but I made sure it was a must for me, day in and day out. I have learned the Devil could come to kill and destroy, and if he took control of your mind, it would be impossible to come back. We must stand on

God's word in all that we do. He never said it would be easy, that's for sure, but it's our job to stay the course and seek His face for direction.

Over the next few years, I grew in His word and in God. I learned to understand why things happen the way they do, which also allowed me to give back to Him. I am able to see a great deal now and have been able to come across a lot of great people because of His word.

I am still in the Extended Stay, and this time, I am getting increasingly tired. I realized I did not have to be there that long, but when you get comfortable somewhere, it is hard to move. I began to seek the face of God and asked Him what He needed me to do. I got to the point where any and every little thing aggravated me. I tried my best not to let it be displayed on my face, but it was nearly impossible as time went on. A lot of changes went into effect at my job that I did not like or want, crazy things were happening at church, and something just had to give. My new boss stepped into the role of the wicked witch of the west and was rude to everyone in sight. She was forced into the role and did not want to be there, so, in retaliation, she went after everyone that she could get her hands on. So, I decided to search for a new job that would treat me better.

Unfortunately, I decided to look for a new role when there were not many options to choose from. After what seemed like forever of searching and applying, I found a new job with a different company. Unfortunately, it came with a pay cut, but I was getting out of a toxic work environment, so I saw it as a win-win situation for me. Even after one good thing that God handed to me, I remained in a dark place.

God asked me, "What is it? I do not understand what it is that you need me to see or do for your kingdom." I stayed in a dark place for what seemed like forever, but realistically only a few months. One thing you should know about me is I love to serve God's people. I will help anyone I can, but the only thing is people will take advantage and leach off you and get what they can from you, no matter if it's your friends, family, or people from your church. I know we all go through tough days; for me, this day was tough for me. I sat in my car during lunch break, and when I began walking back to the building, I overheard a large group of people in the parking lot. I looked around and did not see anything, so as I almost left the parking lot, I stood still as I noticed there was a large group of homeless people behind me, and they were looking for food and water. At that moment, I realized that no matter how tough my day might have been, there were others going through a tougher time. The Bible says in Deuteronomy 15: 7-11, *'If there is among you a poor man of your brethren, within any of the gates in your land which the LORD your God is giving you, you shall not harden your heart nor shut your hand from your poor brother, but you shall open your hand wide to him and willingly lend him sufficient for his need, whatever he needs. Beware let there be a wicked thought in your heart, saying, 'The seventh year, the year of release, is at hand,' and your eye be evil against your poor brother, and you give him nothing, and he cry out to the LORD against you, and it becomes sin among you. You shall surely give to him, and your heart should not be grieved when you give to him, because for this thing the* LORD *your God will bless you in all your works and in all to which you put your hand. For the poor will never cease from the land; therefore, I command you, saying, 'You shall open your hand wide to your brother, to your poor and your needy, in your land.'* When you help your fellow humans, your brothers and sisters in Christ, you are not losing! Instead, you are gaining far more than you can think of. This is from the word of God, and it does not lie. A man that gives to God gains far more than the world.

As I walked back toward the building and in the middle of the parking lot, I began to give God his praises. His will was clear to me once again. SERVE MY PEOPLE. I learned that in all that we do, our job is to serve God's people. If we take care of them, He will take care of us. Just as clear as the sky above me, my vision was crystal. Suddenly, a light bulb turned on in my head. I immediately rushed back to the office, completed my daily tasks, and rushed home.

I asked Him, "God, is this it? Is this what you want me to do?" I laid before Him, asking to make it clear. While lying face-down, the name Sidney Cares Foundation came to me. "Okay, God? Is this what it is going to be?" The more I sought His face, the more things fell into place. I continued, "God, I strongly believe if we show more love, the world would be a better place." Then, the motto "A Gift of Love" is something we all have.

I could not believe it, my own foundation where I could serve His people in ways that I never thought possible. I began to pull things together to make my vision come to light. Though there was not money coming from the outside, I invested my own money to take care of the people of God, as I know He will take care of me. I have fed the homeless numerous times, provided food to many that had homes, furnished complete homes for people who did not have the things they needed in their homes, provided hotel stays, and did anything else I could do to help. For me, it's not about being seen but about doing the work of the Lord and serving His people. Oftentimes, doing this, the spirit would fall on like no other.

This is it…

Chapter 33

Over the next few months, God showed me time and again how much of an impact he has had on my life. In seeking His face, I asked for solitude in a place larger than where I resided. Thankfully, it was temporary. Before I asked Him for a place to stay, I tested the waters. The old saying, "try Jesus; it's nothing like Him," I had a car but was tired of it. It was too small, and I took the easy way out. I had a sit down with God.

"God, this car ain't it. I have had nothing but issues with it." I said to Him.

"You are the one that went out and got it without me. You just jumped in and did your own thing without seeking me first." God replied.

So, I said, "Okay, if that's what you want. You are right, I did, and I am sorry."

"Seek me in all that you do." He told me.

Later, I went home and laid face-down, giving God the quiet time that I promised. On Sunday, I went to church, and a member approached me, "I heard you've been having problems with your car."

I responded, "Yes, but I trust God."

He responded, "There is a member of the church that works for one of the local dealerships, and he wants you to come and talk to him." After service that day, I approached the church member, and he said to visit him at the dealership sometime that next week. That week, I made my way over to the dealership to speak with him and told him how unhappy I was in the car. I told him the basics and that I had no money.

I laid down before God again, "I am here."

"I know," he said.

"Is this a move on your behalf?" I asked.

"I told you to seek my face and trust me, did not I?"

"Yes, but I do not have a down payment."

"I told you to seek my face and trust me."

"I do not want to trade in my car."

God repeated, "I told you to seek my face and trust me."

I asserted, "I want third-row seats, brand new, in gray or black."

He inserted Himself, "NOW LOOK!!"

"Okay, okay."

That Wednesday, I went to the dealership and told the salesperson I had no intention to trade in my car. I knew what I wanted in the next car, I did not have money for a down payment, and I did not want to spend my entire day looking at cars. All the salespersons could do was display a confused look and say, "I will say, you are asking for a whole lot." And after 15 minutes, he pulled up in a green SUV.

Baffled, I asked, "What is that? It's not going to work." I spoke to God, "I thought I said dark gray or black."

"And I said, trust me!" He repeated.

"Okay, okay…" I let things play out.

I hopped in the car, and the salesperson told me, "I had to get you out of the dealership because you walked out. This is not the car we are going to put you in, but it's the same model and year."

I added, "I can deal with that." I drove the green SUV around for a little, and the salesperson's phone rang. They were ready for us to return to the dealership. When I walked into the back office, the salesperson laid out the details of the vehicle on the table. It was everything I asked for. No questions asked. At that moment, I realized I serve an awesome God. I knew that if He did it for me, He would do it for you. I could not believe it, two cars and just like that, I had everything I wanted. Formerly, I walked everywhere I needed to go. I would not let anything, or anyone, stop me from serving my God. After a while, I found myself seeking His voice, "God, you showed out on that, did not you?"

"I always take care of you; all you have to do is seek my face in all that you do."

"You are right," I added, "So, about this house, I want to move into…."

He interrupted, "You are the one that wanted a roommate. You never had one before, so why would you make that move and not seek me first? I provided for you for years and you never needed anything." When you do not seek His face, things like this happen.

"I understand, you are right. I didn't. Well, this place that I am in now is exhausting."

"I told you to seek my face and trust me."

"But I did not think I would qualify to move anywhere. I haven't tried, but I already know they are going to tell me no."

"How do you know already? Are you me?"

"Um, no I am not you, and no I do not know."

"All you have to do is ask and it shall be given. Seek my face and trust me."

"Okay. Well, I want to be in a good area with 3 or 4 bedrooms."

"Here we go again!"

"Okay, okay, okay."

Several weeks passed, and I sought out His face. I listened to His word and applied for the place I wanted. I did not hear back from them, but I did not stop there. When I came across the second place, there weren't any pictures on the website. Something told me to go by there any way to look at it. When I went by the place, I was amazed by how nice the place was.

While mesmerized by what I saw, I could not help but think if I was able to get it. I doubted my eligibility. Over the next several days, I sought his face. "God, I think I found a place, a good place."

"Did you apply for it?" He asked.

"No, I am scared they are going to tell me no, or I will need a cosigner."

"I told you to seek my face and trust me."

"Okay, I got it in my head." The next day, I took the chance and submitted my application. Within 5 minutes, I received an email that I was approved! I could not believe it. "God!!"

"Yes??"

"I know you are probably getting tired of me, but I wanted to thank you."

"I never get tired of hearing from you. This is what I do. I specialize in this kind of stuff."

"Okay, got it!" God continued to bless us in all that we did. When we think things are impossible, He makes them possible. We are all children of the king.

Chapter 34

For as long as I can remember, I have always shared my love for a child. I always wanted children of my own, but the fear of them having to deal with what I've had to overcome has stopped me from doing so. There are generational issues passed down from parents and grandparents. My dad has always been a very heavy alcoholic. I can remember him as a child getting drunk and becoming very violent when he consumed too much. He had a very bad habit of drinking and driving. I recall one day when he got in a high-speed chase with the police. I was sure they were going to kill him. At that time, I was very young, and my dad was my pride and joy. No matter the amount of wrong he did to me, all I wanted was him. I later found out that my grandfather had the same issue my dad had. When he also got drunk, he would become very violent to others around him, family or not. There was one time when my grandfather visited us, and my dad got him drunk. He and my grandmother had exchanged some words, and things took a turn for the worst. My dad had to come and get him, and dad apologized to my grandmother and me for my grandfather's behavior. At that point, I realized this was going to keep happening. They had an illness, a disease, and although alcoholism ran deep in their genes, they could overcome it; I wanted nothing of it, and I chose to stay away from it, any temptation. This was something that was passed down across many generations, the gift of alcohol. Grandfather and dad weren't the only ones that had an issue with alcohol in the family, and I did not want my children to have to deal with this or have to fight this demon. They deserved much more than that.

But still having a heart for children, I had an old high school classmate who had gotten pregnant by one of the guys in the community. Remember my Godson? It was a one-night stand, and at that time, he did not want anything to do with the child. Many times, she had to take care of both of her children on her own with no support. As a young mother who was also dealing with an illness, it was something no parent should go through. There were times when I would take the youngest child to church and keep him with me so she could have time for herself. He became my heart. It was nothing like spoiling a child and being able to give them back, but I began to make sure he had the things he needed. I gave him all the time in the world, he just needed to say the word, and I would be there.

During the time I was in the hospital a few years ago, his mother told me he did not have shoes for school, and unfortunately, I could not leave the hospital to buy him a new pair. I had to call a friend and beg her to get him some shoes for school the next day, and I would pay her back. Although I was very sick, I wanted to make sure he had what he needed for school. As soon as I was released from the hospital, I headed straight to where he was. Nothing else mattered at that time except him. I could only do what I was allowed to do, which was provided for him.

Over time, because there were people who did not really want me to have anything to do with him, I lost connection with the boy. I thought about him, how he was doing, what was going on in his life, if he was okay, if his mother was okay, anything and everything my mind could think of. After many years of not talking or hearing from him, one day, I received a phone call. I learned that he had been sent to his mom's with only a book bag full of clothes and a few personal items. I immediately planned a trip to go and see him, but while I was there, I went to visit my grandmother since she only lived a few hours away.

While there, I enjoyed every moment I got to spend time with him. I let him get anything he wanted when we were out, but I noticed his hesitation. Seeing the look on his face reminded me of myself because I was afraid to be a burden to anyone. He was a very good kid who wanted nothing. I told him, "With me, there is no limit. Go and get whatever you want." I also set up a bank account where I added money and let him use it to get what he wanted whenever he needed it. As I promised to provide for him, I kept my word. Later on, I noticed that the money I transferred into his account would be gone soon after. When looking at the bank statements, the transactions were for things that did not apply to him. As such, people close to him found out and took advantage of the money, spending it on things that were not even for him. And then, on top of the money problem, I heard that he had been missing school because he had issues getting enrolled due to his dad sending his grandmother the wrong paperwork and his grandmother being limited to what she could do. I reached out to his grandmother for help, and her only response was that her hands were tied. She could not get the boy's dad to work with her. I reached out to his father and asked if there was anything I could do to help the boy get back into school, but there was only so much I could do. As a Godparent, my best interest is always the safety and wellbeing of the child if neither parent is able to be there, dead or alive. I reached out to the school, and they said there was nothing that could be done since the paperwork that was sent was not completed.

After several weeks of going back and forth, it was almost two months, and the boy was still not in school. His mother told me she wanted me to help and do what needed to be done. I offered the take him and allow him to stay with me so I could get him in school, and he would visit his parents on holidays and vacations. She and his grandmother agreed to this arrangement. I told them I would get an attorney to help with everything, so if there was an issue, we would have taken the proper steps. They asked that I get custody of both him and his older brother, who was also having issues. We talked about the other brother living with his grandmother and mother based on the current situation. I felt it was best for him to live in a smaller city where he could get into less trouble with his grandmother and mother by his side.

Over the next several weeks, an attorney was hired, and several trips were made from Pennsylvania to North Carolina. We had to sign mountains of paperwork and transferring of files had taken place until one day, the child was set to go to school the following Monday. I reached out to the local charter school, one of the best in the community, so that when the lottery opened, he would be able to get in. The following weeks were pure hell, but I never let my Godson see it on my face. I had spent well over six-thousand dollars to try and make sure he had what he needed so he could get into school. Since his mother did not have the money to support him, I upfronted the funds. In a way, I think he knew that I was going to take care of him and make sure he had what he needed. His grandmother and I eventually revisited the conversation about the oldest brother coming to live with her, and I kept the youngest one. Unfortunately, she did not want this and asked me to keep the oldest child and send the youngest brother back up with her.

I explained to her that I lived in a much bigger city, and it would be more dangerous for him there. It was gut-wrenching to deny a little boy a safe place to stay, but I knew in my heart that it was the right thing to do. I had to stand my ground for what was right.

I took the youngest child to the store and got him all the food he liked to eat. Like all kids, he instinctively picked a lot of junk food and sweets. I explained to him that he needed to eat real, good, nutritious food, and I would allow him to get some junk food as long as he agreed to eat some veggies also. I noticed that he was not sleeping at night but playing all-nighters on video games. This was a habit he formed from staying with his grandmother. I explained to him that when school started, he would not be able to stay up all night and play video games, especially on school nights.

When Sunday morning arrived, he had not been with me a full week yet. I woke up at about 6:30 am and noticed his door was shut and locked. Because he was not sleeping, I would often check on him throughout the night to make sure he was okay. I asked and waited for him to unlock and open the door and asked him if he was okay and why he had the door locked, and he responded, "Yes, I am fine."

I said, "Okay, I just wanted to check on you."

"I just finished playing the game." He replied, and I simply said OKAY. I went on about my business. About an hour later, I received a phone call from his grandmother, saying he wanted to come and live with her, saying he missed her and wanted to come back up there with her. I asked her if there was something wrong or if something had happened, and she said no, he just missed his grandmother. At this point, I realized she was pissed off and got to the boy's head and manipulated him to want to come back.

I immediately knew I had to pull myself together. Everything that I had sacrificed to make sure he had what he needed and wanted felt like a waste, and I had been taken advantage of. I asked him what brought this on or what happened, and he stated that he talked to his grandmother this morning, and she wanted him back up there with her. He did not want me to feel any type of way, and I told him that if he did not want to be there, he did not have to stay there. Whatever made him happy is what he should do, and I would be there for him. I told him to pack everything he brought with him, and I would take him back to his grandmother's.

I realized that because she could not run my house the way she thought, she could use the child to get what she wanted, so she thought. But it does not ever work like that. I will do whatever it takes to help him, but once I feel like my help is being taken advantage of, I will pull back. As we began to travel up the highway, I began to think about how I had traveled up and down this same highway, hours after hours, and I was not going to do it again for someone that was not grateful. I told him I would take him back to his dad's house, who lived about 30 minutes away. He begged me not to take him there and asked if he could just go back to my house, but I explained to him that he did not want to be at my house and instead wanted to be with his grandmother. I told him that he would need to work it out with his dad. He did not like that arrangement, but at this point, he had no choice but to deal with it. His grandmother was pissed that she did not get what she wanted at that time, but I was done with the whole thing at that point. She now had to learn how to figure out what lie she could make up to make herself look good. At that point, I did not care what she did or did not do. I was pulling away. The one thing I took out of this; Just to remember every dog has its day.

Chapter 35

W hile I tried to help my Godson, I was in contact with my grandmother. We spoke several times, but we never saw each other. In family photos, I was never seen there, and she had wondered why. My mother would tell her that I was visiting my dad, yet oftentimes when my mom spoke to my grandmother, she always asked her where I was; she told her I was visiting, lying as usual. Grandmother never knew my mom gave me away. She was her usual self, spitting out lies.

When I drove to see her for the first time, we both had questions about the middleman who continuously spouted out lies to make herself look good and establish the "perfect mother" image. I told grandma that mom was never active or present in my life, and between the ages of 2 and 20, I only saw her maybe, 5 times. I will never forget the look of disbelief she had on her face. All this time, my mother's side of my family never knew the real truth. This whole time, my dad's mom had been carrying the load, making sure I had what I needed. On the other hand, I also discovered grandma went through a lot of pain herself. It's disappointing that many times in life, people look down on us because their life did not end up the way they wanted them to be. We all have things we need to work on, some more than others. We should use them to build up and make them better.

Meeting my grandmother was one of the best moments that happened to me. In a state of depression, she made everything okay. If I am ever having a day, a simple phone call from her always makes it better. At times, I found myself wanting to just be in her presence because spending time with the people you love, especially a grandmother, is something I will always cherish.

My friend's birthday arrived, and she wanted to go out of town to celebrate. I did not have the money to go, especially after recently being in a car accident; funds were extremely tight. My friend has been a huge blessing; basically, she's my unrelated little sister. We always had a fun time together, and I knew that it was struggle for me to go out of town to celebrate her birthday. But I did not want to let her down.

At first, she wanted me to fly, but I knew the better option would be to drive with a friend. I offered one of my friends to ride with me, with the help of contributing to gas. Thankfully, he was down to help. What was most surprising was that she was engaged to be married, even though she had been with this one guy for almost 10 years, but not the one she was marrying. Apparently, there was another guy about 6 months earlier than she was seeing and talking about while she was in the relationship with the other guy. Where did this new guy come from? I knew her best friend got engaged recently, and I did not want to think the only reason she was getting married was because of her best friend was getting married and she was rushing to get married before her to prove a point.

. But several questions arose as to why she would rush to get married to a guy she had been with for only 3 months. But we moved on, and I tried my best to plan something nice for her birthday. I ordered a cake. Other than buying dessert, I did not know what else was happening. I asked her what we would do, where we would go, and how things would be done. I did not want to waste time and sit around all day. The only activity on the list was going to a bar crawl, which was not ideal; however, I pushed onward on the exhausting 11-hour drive. As the trip continued, the stress began to add on, and my eyes felt heavy. My body was desperate to fight off exhaustion, so we played phone tag.

Eventually, it got late enough, and I pulled over to sleep and did not realize she kept calling me. And then when I woke up, I called her, and she would not answer. We finally arrived, and she felt some type of way. When I asked why she was upset, she said it was because I would not answer her calls. I immediately defended myself and told her that I had to pull off the highway to catch up on sleep. She would not listen to my "excuse" and ignored my reasoning. I decided to move on and enjoy the night.

When I went to pick up the cake at 1:30 pm, I did not know what was going on next. So, we went over to her hotel room and saw her family come on the trip as well. I set up the birthday cake in her room, and I checked the time and saw it was 4:00 pm, finally realizing the last time I had food was at 8:00 am. I approached her and told her that we were all starving, so we headed over to a restaurant, and by the time we got there, there was a wait – go figure. And if there was not anything to complicate it even further, her cousin called to cancel because she was not going to make it on time. At this point, we were all starving, but the restaurant informed us they would not have our table ready until almost 2 hours later. She called her family to let them know of the 2-hour wait, and since they wanted to eat there too, we continued to wait.

My stomach began to take over my mouth when I said, "This is not fair to us. We need to eat, and we have been waiting all day, even after driving all this way, dressing up, and doing everything you wanted. Not to mention, we are sitting and waiting in the heat!" This was when it hit me that there was basically no plan to any of this – no one knew what was going on anymore. And finally, after waiting 2 hours, at 7:00 pm, we made it to the restaurant. I kept thinking to myself, *'The food better be delicious.'* Once we sat down, I found out that the food was cooked together in this God-forsaken restaurant. What in the hell did I loop myself into? So, because I do not eat chicken, beef, or pork, I was going to be forced to eat it and feel the wrath from my stomach later. Finally, we were sitting at a table two hours later, and there was nothing I could eat. I was most definitely over it by now. We had already wasted a full day, and I had not eaten much except eggs from the morning, but clearly, it was not holding me up by now. What pissed me off more was that I continuously asked what the plan was, and the only answer I seemed to receive was crickets. All I knew was that tomorrow was going to be my last day, and we did not do anything but go to this restaurant where the menu was everything I could not eat.

By this time, she was over me, and I was over her. I think it's selfish she made us wait on others without taking others' time into consideration, family or not. You do not do that. When they finished eating, we went back to the bars, which was the last thing I wanted to do since my body was hot and starving from the lack of food it had received. My body began to shake since the last time it had real food was early that morning. But out of some crazy, insane thinking that went through my head, I pushed forward with the minimal energy my body had left. When we got to the bar, I immediately sat at the closest table to rest my feet, exhausted. My friend asked me to get up to walk around, but all I wanted to do was leave and go to sleep. Being me, however, I pushed forward. We made our way back to the bar where our friends were, and once I sat on the chair near the tables, my body decided it was time to get rest.

My body was so drained from everything I did not even realize I kept falling asleep. When I woke up, everyone was doing their own thing—embarrassment was displayed across my face. She looked at me and stated that I was acting funny for needing to lay down, but I was not acting funny at all. I just wanted to go to the room and fall asleep. Later, I finally got food elsewhere.

The next morning, I told my friend I booked a swamp ride at 3:00 pm. While everyone was at the restaurant, eating and having a grand time the day before, I booked the swamp ride since I could not eat the food and had nothing else to do. As a favor beforehand, she asked me to pick her up from the hotel she was at and take her to a new one. Apparently, she decided to change rooms, which I did not mind helping with. Then when she found out, it was just for me and my homeboy who was there with me, she told me she was pissed and accused me of only thinking about myself.

When I jumped in to defend myself, saying that if people decided to sleep into 3 to 4 o'clock in the afternoon, that's on them. But apparently, because it's her birthday, everything that anyone does has to be about her. That's not how life works. After I went through to get to her, she could at least be gracious enough to say thank you.

When she found out I was going on the swamp ride without her or her family, she was angry, assuming I selfishly and purposefully left them out of the equation. She added more gasoline to the fire, saying I should have asked beforehand and how I should have been considerate, and on and on she went. Prior before the trip ever happened, I asked her multiple times about the swamp ride and never got a clear answer from her. A massive blowup for no reason. I called the place that was hosting the swamp ride and asked if they had 2 more seats available for her and her friend, and thankfully, they worked it out; however, by this point, she was trying to prove a point and did not want me to pick her up.

This place was over forty-five minutes away from their hotel, so now they are putting themselves in a pickle where they needed to take a rideshare. But oh well, I went on with my homeboy and made it there on time. They, on the other hand, because of her whining, complaining, and toddler-aged temper tantrum she pulled, arrived when the boats pulled off the dock, making them lose their money. The unfortunate part was they had to spend even more money to take rideshare back.

Later, she called me while I was trying to enjoy my swamp ride and asked me what the plan was for the evening. At that moment, I was just focusing on the swamp ride because when I tried to think about what type of plan was on the docket for the evening, would be plans that would be a repeat of the restaurant I could not eat at. To prevent myself from remembering that night, I presented my ideas, and she inserted what she wanted to do so everyone was on the same page. Thankfully, I chose to put my energy toward things more positively and made it a point not to focus on the negative around me.

Even though we fought and wanted to pull each other's hair out, she was like a sister to me, and I wanted to make sure she was making the right decision, especially since she stated that every lady this guy had been with never treated him right; that was a red flag to me, but I refrained from saying anything. I can see that if they were able to get together and, in a year, got married, it would be understandable. But after only 3 months, it seemed a bit off, but that's what she was pushing for, and if anyone had something to say about it, she deleted them from her life. Even members of her family were questioning her decision, but she ignored them. I could not understand that.

Apparently, this new guy was in the service, which was her reasoning for getting married so soon; I mean, it made sense a lot of couples who are in the service do it. So, I asked her if she was marrying him for the military benefits, you get when in the service, and she took that offensively. So, if that was the case, I could understand why she was rushing to get married. However, she denied that was the reason. I said OKAY and moved on.

A week passed by, and my phone rang; it was her. She attacked me, accusing me of offending and disrespecting her by asking what I did…more than a week ago. I did not understand why she held onto that for so long when she could have just come to me. I had just left church, I was in a good mood, and now I had to deal with this, more drama. Instantly, I told her my plan was not to offend her or anything like that. I apologized profusely, but she remained stuck on the one question that apparently turned into this "life-threatening" issue.

Although the pain was too much, I realized that in God's times, everything happens for a reason. We want things and people to stay with us for a lifetime. Sometimes, that's not the plan. Sometimes, people come into your life to teach you something. That's okay, too. We can take every bad thing and let it take control of our lives, or we can let it come to an end and move on. I hate how things happened the way they did. My prayer was that God protected her in all that she did.

Chapter 36

*N*ow *Moses was tending the flock of Jethro his father-in-law, the priest of Midian, and he led the flock to the far side of the wilderness and came to Horeb, the mountain of God. There the angel of the* LORD *appeared to him in flames of fire from within a bush. Moses saw that though the bush was on fire it did not burn up. So, Moses's thought, "I will go over and see this strange sight—why the bush does not burn up."*

When the LORD *saw that he had gone over to look, God called to him from within the bush, "Moses! Moses!"*

And Moses said, "Here I am."

"Do not come any closer," God said. "Take off your sandals, for the place where you are standing is holy ground." Then he said, "I am the God of your father, the God of Abraham, the God of Isaac, and the God of Jacob." At this, Moses hid his face, because he was afraid to look at God.

The LORD *said, "I have indeed seen the misery of my people in Egypt. I have heard them crying out because of their slave drivers, and I am concerned about their suffering. So, I have come down to rescue them from the hand of the Egyptians and to bring them up out of that land into a good and spacious land, a land flowing with milk and honey—the home of the Canaanites, Hittites, Amorites, Perizzites, Hivites, and Jebusites. And now the cry of the Israelites has reached me, and I have seen the way the Egyptians are oppressing them. So now, go. I am sending you to Pharaoh to bring my people the Israelites out of Egypt." But Moses said to God, "Who am I that I should go to Pharaoh and bring the Israelites out of Egypt?"*

And God said, "I will be with you. And this will be the sign to you that it is I who have sent you: When you have brought the people out of Egypt, you will worship God on this mountain."

Moses said to God, "Suppose I go to the Israelites and say to them, 'The God of your fathers has sent me to you,' and they ask me, 'What is his name?' Then what shall I tell them?"

God said to Moses, "I AM WHO I AM. This is what you are to say to the Israelites: 'I AM has sent me to you.'"

God also said to Moses, "Say to the Israelites, 'The LORD, the God of your fathers—the God of Abraham, the God of Isaac, and the God of Jacob—has sent me to you.'

"This is my name forever,

the name you shall call me

from generation to generation.

"Go, assemble the elders of Israel and say to them, 'The LORD, the God of your fathers—the God of Abraham, Isaac and Jacob – appeared to me and said: I have watched over you and have seen what has been done to you in Egypt. And I have

promised to bring you up out of your misery in Egypt into the land of the Canaanites, Hittites, Amorites, Perizzites, Hivites, and Jebusites – a land flowing with milk and honey.'

"The elders of Israel will listen to you. Then you and the elders are to go to the king of Egypt and say to him, 'The LORD, the God of the Hebrews, has met with us. Let us take a three-day journey into the wilderness to offer sacrifices to the LORD our God.' But I know that the king of Egypt will not let you go unless a mighty hand compels him. So, I will stretch out my hand and strike the Egyptians with all the wonders that I will perform among them. After that, he will let you go.

"And I will make the Egyptians favorably disposed toward this people so that when you leave you will not go empty-handed. Every woman is to ask her neighbor and any woman living in her house for articles of silver and gold and for clothing, which you will put on your sons and daughters. And so, you will plunder the Egyptians."

A lot of people may not know, but it takes a lot of courage to live life. You hear lots of people say things like 'when life throws lemons at you, you make lemonades out of it' but they forget how very difficult it is. They say it like it can be achieved by just anybody at any time but that is not true; it is false! I am saying this because I have seen how very hard it is to stand up from nothingness and make something out of it. In the bible passage above, many people only see the power of God at work in Moses, and I see that too. But there is one more thing that I see; I see a man who is willing and ready to change his life and use that change to impact the people around him in such a powerful and positive way. Listen, it is not an easy task to lead people, you know? When you lead people, or when you agree to lead people, you are taking complete responsibility for their lives. You are saying that you are willing to be held responsible for their day-to-day activities, their health, their mistakes and errors, and their well-being. This is not an easy task. Moses was a stammerer; he was not physically prepared for such a task. If there was a weighing scale to determine who would be fit to be a leader, he would not have reached half of the requirement. But God is not a man. The Bible says in 1 Samuel 16:7 *'But the LORD said to Samuel, "Do not consider his appearance or his height, for I have rejected him. The LORD does not look at the things people look at. People look at the outward appearance, but the LORD looks at the heart."'* What keeps a man strong is in his heart, never in the outward appearance. Did you know that one's outward appearance is not just one's physique? It also includes everything that is eternal of you. It includes the many years of being bullied, experiences of hate, distrust, broken families, absence of help from close ones, and having no shoulder to lean on when things get too tough to handle. I have seen all of these and more, yet I have stayed strong even until now. What has kept me strong for the last 36 years of my life is what is in my heart, not outside of it. God lets us know that what we have on the insides of ourselves is far greater than what is on the outside and I could not agree less.

God is divine, and he sees far more than we can. When he has plans for you, nothing can stand in the way. For Moses, we can see how he really thought that he needed to be an eloquent speaker to be used by God, and of course, I understand this. It is like being told to fight in a boxing competition when you weigh less than 150 pounds. It is crazy and anyone who hears it will laugh. But listen, God has such big plans for you so when he tells you to move, you better move! I could have been distraught and hopeless with everything that happened around me, starting from my parents to my experience with friends, neighbors, colleagues, and family members; it is such a long list of 'but'. I decided to add another 'but' against all other buts and say to it 'but God said this to me!'

Across the past 36 years, the most difficult challenge I have had to face was to focus on myself. Often, I have found myself putting others first before focusing on what I need. Unfortunately, I learned this the hard way from having people constantly pull and stretch the taffy I had to offer; taffy can only stretch so far before there is nothing left to give. I was forced to learn the word 'No.' I have a true heart, and I never fail to wear it on my sleeve for anyone, no matter the situation. In every situation I faced or dealt with, I have remained humble and sought out God's face for comfort and serenity.

People from both the streets and church will do what they can to make themselves look good to the outside world. They will lie and cover up the dirt that is on their face with the best undercover disguise they can fool others with. Remember, this is about them, not God. When a situation is no longer affiliated with Him, remove yourself from it all.

I believe that God assigns us both what we can handle and have to push ourselves to achieve. We are meant to seek His face and get a clear understanding of what we need to do to complete His assignment. The assignment will have something to do with a significant role in your life, whether it be your job, your home, and your church, whatever. Before you move to seek His face and stay the course, complete the assignment at hand. Once He closes the door, somehow, He opens a nearby window. As I say, "Stand still until His will is clear."

I've learned to focus more on myself by letting go of people or things that delivered nothing but negative, toxic energy. We, as people, should take time to see where we have room for growth. In some cases, that may mean identifying the poor habits we have collected from previous experiences, and a way to find that is to sit back and conduct a self-evaluation to see where we have gone wrong. Listen; no one is perfect; we all have room for growth. I've traveled to so many places I never imagined I would visit.

Here is a little word of advice: no matter what you do, start to take time out of your day and week for yourself. I know we have all heard this more times than we can count, but you truly do only live once. Why waste it? A simple, early morning of work or an overnight getaway helps me relax and see what I need to do better for myself. Plan a weeklong trip for yourself and get away from the daily stresses life brings because, at the end of the day, they'll be awaiting your return. Regroup and find what you need to strive for excellence.

Take the time to set your goals of where you want to be in life and write them down. You have such a long way ahead of you. Yes, you have God, but you must be ready. Do not forget that this can be something to work towards, and do not ever allow anyone to stop you from getting there. If there is something stopping you from getting to the next level in life, let it go; it's not worth it, seriously. If your friends and family are holding you back or failing to understand that you are striving for excellence, pull away. I've learned that it's every man for himself, and some people just do not want to see you happy. It's pathetically true. They are looking to see what they can do to pull you down and destroy the inner happiness you get to build. And in the end, even if you try to tell them what they are doing wrong, let them go. Focus on you; you are worth more.

Chapter 37

I would like to tell you a short story from the Bible to close this. It is the story of the wife of a prophet of God who had just lost her husband. The Bible says in 2 Kings 4: 1-7:

'The wife of a man from the company of the prophets cried out to Elisha, "Your servant my husband is dead, and you know that he revered the LORD. But now his creditor is coming to take my two boys as his slaves."

Elisha replied to her, "How can I help you? Tell me, what do you have in your house?"

"Your servant has nothing there at all," she said, "except a small jar of olive oil."

Elisha said, "Go around and ask all your neighbors for empty jars. Don't ask for just a few. Then go inside and shut the door behind you and your sons. Pour oil into all the jars, and as each is filled, put it to one side."

She left him and shut the door behind her and her sons. They brought the jars to her, and she kept pouring. When all the jars were full, she said to her son, "Bring me another one."

But he replied, "There is not a jar left." Then the oil stopped flowing.

She went and told the man of God, and he said, "Go, sell the oil and pay your debts. You and your sons can live on what is left."'

There is a very big lesson to learn from this story and I would need you to be ready to understand and apply it because I know I would not have come this far without it. One of the biggest lessons that I have learned in my life is this; God can do it, but if a man refuses to obey, then He would not do it. The wife of the prophet was knee-deep in debt! One may say 'Oh, God should have taken care of her since her husband was his servant' but we must understand that each person has their own battles in this thing called life. I was born to people who did not show me much love and care, so I would not tell God to pass on their 'blessings' unto me simply because I am their child, no! I planted my feet on the ground and found my way around life. It was not easy and though these are just writings, I tell you for sure that not everyone would be able to survive the battle I went through and am still going through. From the story above, we can see that God had blessings waiting for the woman and her family, he just needed them to show that they were ready to receive. If they had not gotten as many bowls as they could, they would not have been able to receive as much as God was ready to give them. Do you see this?

Another thing is note is that the oil did not stop flowing until they said they had no other jars left. What does that say? You will only receive as many blessings as you are able and ready to receive. Many times, people cry and complain about their situation in life. They claim that they were born into poor circumstances that are not favorable and because of that, they are still on the ground. While this may be considered true, I do not agree with such a narrative, and this is why; some people are born into very comfortable situations, and they run it all down to zero. I have seen in my life that as long as a person is ready to change their life, nothing can stop them. Your experiences may push you back to the ground and hurt you badly but rather than stay down, get back up each time and let your past stay where it belongs; in the past!

Many times, in life, we wonder why things happen. Then sometimes, you find yourself looking up to the sky and yelling, "Why me?!" Why have I been the one to endure the unending pain and suffering? Over the past 37 years of my life, I have learned that feeling pain, suffering, loss, grief, and agony are a part of life. There are things that had I not gone through when I did, and I would not be who I am or where I am today. Let's face it; I could have gone through much worse, or I could have thrown in the towel and given up. There were several moments where I wanted to just end it all and be done; Shut the door, turn off the light, and let myself fade away into oblivion. But what strengthened me was remembering that God would never put on us more than we could bear. If there is something I am going through now, more than likely, it's a chance it going to occur again. And when we look at the family and friends we have connected with or become close to, I've learned that everything we go through is with someone we love. I've found myself stepping in as a support system for the ones I love. Not everyone can endure the things we go through in life. Frankly, not everyone deserves it. God surely has a way of sending His strongest Angels to fight the toughest battles.

If we simply choose to use the things that were set up to hurt us the most, then it will prevent us from rising to where we need to be. There are times when God will put you in places to fight battles that others can't handle. He will also put us all in place to learn from our mistakes. An example is when a couple does everything, they can save their marriage but do nothing but fight on a constant basis. In this case, no matter how hard they both tried, everything they learned in their marriage will move on with them.

In my life, I have had a network of friends, some still here and some parted ways. Not every friendship was a good one, let's not forget that, but I appreciate the connections I made. Even if it was a simple conversation we had or an experience we advanced, I always took something good from it. On the other hand, there are people called leeches who will use you for what they can. It's sad to say, but all 37 years of my life, I have met good and kind-hearted people like myself, but I have also met some people who take advantage of my kindness and use them for their own gain. But I have kept my head held high.

One of my greatest challenges has been dealing with rejection. Many do not understand the pain and the hurt a child can confront when they are rejected by a family member or friend because of the color of his skin or a family that did not want anything to do with the child because his mother did not want him. It's even worse when most of your life, growing up, that child never knew his mother's side of the family, and after the passing of his grandmother, he becomes a black sheep on his father's side. I grew up hearing that "It's nothing like family." That's your blood. But the most genuine ones who have shown me what family is are bonded, not from blood. Those people have provided me with some of the most encouraging words, and if I ever needed anything, they had my back no matter what. I will forever be grateful for that. If you were to ask my dad's side of the family why there has been no connection between them and me, the only response you would get is they did not know anything of it, that I was just acting, and would refuse to tell you how they treated me.

But even as a child, after my grandmother passed away, there was a multitude of things I had to face on my own. On July 4th, at 13 years old, I was baptized in the church; I was so excited and told my family, thinking they would be there, only to know that they did not show up. There was no one there for me. No one at all. I thought, "Maybe they are just busy and could not make it." Then when it came to my High School graduation, they didn't really support it either. Countless times there were family events that I was never told about or, for lack of a better word, invited to. The most depressing part is if a family member got sick or passed away, my phone never rang. I was left with no choice but to find out from people on the street or through social media, just like a child reaching out for a hot stove after being burned so many times over and over.

I learned to stay away. I accepted my place in their family, and at this point in my life, I am fine with it. The expectation they have given is that I am not a part of them, and I understand now that I will never be. It is rejection, and it's something that is incredibly hard to deal with. No one wants to deal with rejection. It sucks, but we never know what someone is going through or has been through in life. But why should we let it stop us from living our life to the fullest? Why let it stop you from living? All it takes is one person in a family or a group to not like you and have it spread like Corona.

The best part of this family thing, however, is when I got to meet my grandmother on my mother's side and discovered she was once rejected as well. Seeing her for the first time was amazing as she welcomed me with open arms and never failed to show me what unconditional love was. It was almost like the hurt and pain that we had both been through was voided out, and all we needed was each other. We both understood what we went through, and even though I lost my grandmother on my dad's side and the hole she left will never be filled, my grandmother on my mom's side has shown me so much love I never got to experience before. Even though I am not her only grandchild, her other grandchildren chose not to deal with her because of what's been instilled in their heads; it's okay because I get to keep it all for myself. I will forever be a grandma's boy; there is nothing like the love of a grandmother.

Remember, even in the darkest of situations; there is a light at the end of the tunnel. God has a plan for you, put all of your trust in Him. Give Him the wheel and when He directs you into the jungle, do not be afraid. Just like me, you can walk in through one end of the jungle as a kitten and come out the other end as a lion. It all depends on how much you are willing to learn on the way. Slow down and take things one step at a time.

Right now, it may look so different from how you have always dreamed of it to be, but you are growing and believe me, it is all that matters. Just like the wife of the prophet and his sons, position yourself in a way that you are ready to receive from God. Do not be caught up in the claws of the devil; he will do anything and everything to throw you back in the den and laugh at you when you fall, but he will fail if you turn your back on him and put your focus in your strength in God. Gather your thoughts and move with precision, avoid pleasures that do not last. They are gifts straight from the pit of hell and will bring so much more trouble than good. When you do all of these, I promise that you are going to make it through. God loves you, and so do I. Go forth and emerge in greatness!

Made in the USA
Columbia, SC
20 September 2022

67649891R00107